Chapter 1

'Santa! Santa! Santa you great big loon, we need you in the workshop' The guitar music that could be heard from the other side of the old wooden door came to a halt and there was a muttering of annoyance. The door then swung open and their stood Santa. He took up the whole doorway. His presence was majestic and beautiful, from his black boots with a golden strap that glistened off every bauble, up his red trousers to his luscious red coat. The coat was open and under it Santa simply wore a vest. Tattoos adorned his chest with Holly, mistletoe and his beloved reindeer on show.

The head elf looked up at his face. It was almost square, his beard white but flecked with black, covered his face but was fairly short. A contrast to his long flowing hair. It had made its way to half way down his back and seemed to resemble an old lion's mane. Just like what his face showed, it looked battle worn but still carried a sense of beauty.

'Hey Paul what have I told you about interrupting my flow. You know I need my time playing the guitar with the band'.

Paul automatically chirped back 'well you are still no good after 200 years so I don't see what this interruption would change'

Santa was taken aback by the remark and Paul had even surprised himself on his quick wit. Before either could respond a clang could be heard down the hallway.

Paul carried on 'We have an issue down in the workshop and only you can fix it. The tuners for all the guitars don't work. If we can't get them to work soon then all the children who asked for a guitar for Christmas won't get one'

Santa lost all annoyance from his face and turned his head towards the room he was in 'ok group duty calls, you all keep at it and I shall be back soon'

As Santa shut the door behind him the sounds of guitars, bass and drums could be heard. They both walked down the hall towards the workshop. Santa's great big frame towered over Paul's petite size.

Paul glanced at Santa twice and opened his mouth but no words were produced. On the second time Santa clocks him.

Santa 'What is it?'

Paul 'Nothing it's nothing'

Santa 'That means its playing on your mind then. Come on Paul, spill'

Paul 'I don't like you taking the elves away from their posts, at anytime but especially at Christmas'

Santa 'So would you rather they worked like brain dead robots just making toys twenty-four seven?'

Paul 'Well it would help our performance figures wouldn't it'

Santa 'But that is not what Christmas is about, darn performance figures. Those workers in there are elves not failing numbers on a spreadsheet. They need joy and happiness too. If they feel that in their hearts, it will be in the toys and that is how we can spread Christmas cheer'

Paul 'But Christmas cheer is down to eighty nine percent'

Santa 'Well their we go, not to worry that's an improvement on last year'

Paul 'Yes, but before then we hadn't been below ninety five percent for over one hundred and fifty years'

Santa stopped and turned to look at Paul 'Look, I know it's low but we will bounce back'

Paul 'I, I just need you to take this seriously, Ok Santa. No messing around I need you to make the elves work hard. It is a crazy messed up world out there beyond the north pole. Their maybe happiness and joy but there is a lot of sadness and misery too. I just need to know that you still care and that you still have that Christmas spirit'.

Santa 'We've known each other over what is it six hundred, seven hundred years now right Paul' Paul Nods 'I still care today, just as much as I did the first time I dawned this coat'

Paul 'Then why are you playing heavy metal rock music on Christmas eve? Why are you not making sure the workshop is fine at all times?'

Santa took a deep breath and looked at Paul and a smile broke across his face 'Because my deer fellow I truly believe that heavy metal and music in general is the gateway to the soul. There is nothing quite so pure'.

They both looked at each other for a moment that seemed to last longer. A smile eventually cracked on Paul's face. He then deepened his voice, trying to sound bossy but clearly failing. 'Come on I can't have you being philosophical in the hallway all day, you got to fix those tuners'

*

As they stepped inside the workshop it was like stepping into another magical world. The room was as long as the eye could see. And so tall it touched the sky. Millions of toys were being finalised ready for delivery. Teddy bears flew through the air on to the conveyor belts, the small electric cars danced around their feet and dolls were having their final stiches. Over each section was a great large sign adorned with red and gold tinsel sporting the name of the department in big bold green letters. And finally, in the middle of it all was a tree. But not just any Christmas tree. This was the biggest and most beautiful tree ever to be seen. On it was baubles that represented each country in the world and resting on top, just visible from the bottom was a bright and shining gold star.

Paul gestured to Santa towards the archway which adorned the sign' Musical Instruments'

'If you go in their Bobby will show you the problem'.

*

Inside the department, Santa looked down at the tuner on the guitar which was laid out on the table in front of him. At first glance it looked perfectly normal. Bobby peered over his shoulder slowly and stared at the guitar with him. Bobby explained 'See it may look fine but its not working, the moment I try to play the guitar with it the strings snap and it makes horrible noises'

Santa quipped back 'Are you sure the that's not just your guitar skills'

Bobby turned his head to look at Santa who returned the favour. He stared at Santa for a second before looking at the tuner on the table. 'No, it's definitely the tuner'

Santa looked back down but he was not convinced 'Let's just test it out first' Santa said, as he stood up with the guitar in hand, ready to play.

Bobby began backing off from Santa 'I would advise against that Santa'. He stated nervously.

Santa laughed 'It's only a guitar Bobby'

He strummed the guitar once and it let out a horrible sound which screeched across the room, as all the strings snapped off and all the elves moaned and covered their ears. Santa looked down at the guitar in silence for a moment, then he looked at Bobby who stared back at him in judgement.

'I better fix this hadn't I?'

Bobby nodded slowly.

*

Santa sat at the table, once again started to inspect the tuner on the guitar, whilst Bobby watched over his shoulder. He then proceeded to work at lightening pace, his hands moving so fast they became a blur as Bobby watched on in awe.

A few moments passed and then Santa stopped, Bobby went to move forward but Santa raised his hand 'Wait a sec' Santa slowly tightened the last string of the guitar.

'I think that's done'. He declared.

'Are you sure?' Bobby queried.

'Well their only one way to find out, let's give it a test run'.

Santa then proceeded to stand up and make a few initial strums of the guitar with no disaster. Bobby breathed a sigh of relief while Santa shrugged his shoulder as if to say it was no big issue.

'Thanks for that Santa. Now if you could show me how you fix them and I can get all fifty thousand of our guitars finished'

Santa had a menacing grin appear on his face 'O bobby you can't just play a few chords and be satisfied it's fine. We need a quick jamming session'. He looked over to a number of elves working in the corner and shouted to them 'Elves! Grab these guitars on the wall behind me. Its time for some Christmas classics!' The elves all enthusiastically ran over to the wall to grab guitars and Bobby raised his arms in defeated protest'

With several of the elves with guitars in hand, Santa quickly went past each one fixing each at break neck speed. In this time a small crowd of elves had gathered by the archway to watch the proceedings that would flow. Santa was proud looking at all the elves guitars in hand. To him there was no better site at all and he could not wait to deliver all these guitars so that the children could feel what it was like to play.

Santa's voice now boomed over the room as he spoke 'ok everyone, 1, 2, 1, 2, 3, 4!'

They all began in perfect harmony playing jingle bells, which on the electric guitars, boomed around the whole workshop and ass it came to the chorus Santa began to sing.

'Oh, jingle bells, jingle bells

Jingle all the way

Oh, what fun it is to ride

In a one-horse open sleigh

Hey!'

At this point Paul was at the front of the crowd and Santa clocked his gaze as he looked on disapprovingly.

'Come on Paul it's your favourite. Sing along with us.'

Paul tried to continue to look stern, the elves were supposed to be working after all and well Santa was setting a bad example. But he couldn't. His sternness moved way for happiness, as he got close to the group someone threw him a guitar and he began to play as they belted out the rest of the chorus.

'Jingle bells, Jingle bells

Jingle all the way'

Oh, what fun it is to ride

In a one-horse open sleigh'

Chapter 2

In wales a young man sat at his bedroom window and watched as the snow fell. It had been a few years since he had seen a white Christmas and this looked like one to remember. The snow was thick on the ground and continued to fall down heavily. It covered all the trees and turned the rolling green hills completely white.

Harry didn't really care about Christmas anymore though. He felt it was just for little kids who still believed in Santa and he was 17. How stupid could these kids be? It's not like they put down socks or one of those disgusting Christmas jumpers on their Christmas list but you could be sure that every Christmas morning those presents would be under the tree, ready to be opened to disappointment.

He hadn't always been like this though. Growing up Harry had loved Christmas and got so excited every year. He would make a Christmas cake with his mum, put up the lights and decorations with his dad and he would go Christmas shopping with his older brother and sister, armed with his pocket money ready to find the best present he could with all of his five-pound pocket money. But those days were long gone. Both his siblings had moved out and weren't coming home for Christmas. The decorations were up and the Turkey was in the oven but any feel of Christmas cheer was hollow.

The only thing that brought Harry any cheer was his music. He loved his heavy metal. He would listen to it all day on an old vinyl player that his brother had given him. It just sounds better on here he would tell him. Harry wasn't sure but he loved it anyway and he played all the classics on their that he could find 'Black Sabbath, Led Zeppelin, Motorhead, Metallica, Slayer, slipknot, AC/DC, Jimi Hendrix and so many more. He would just spend hours laying on his bed listening to the music. His eyes shut, imaging things far beyond these four walls.

There was however something else that made Harry happy or more accurately someone and that someone was Jess. She was the most beautiful person that Harry had ever known. She had beautiful platinum hair that reminded Harry of the snow, green emerald eyes, and she wore a nose ring on her button nose. She loved her heavy metal too and that was how they met. Harry had been listening to a song by Metallica when Jess over heard from down the school corridor and they began to talk. Harry couldn't believe his luck and they soon realised they had many things in common and they fell in love with each other. He loved her laugh. She loved his smile. They would go to gigs and then then talk until sunrise afterwards about how it made them feel. To him she was perfect. And to her he was.

As Harry continued to look down the hill from his window, he began to see a figure come into view, as it drew near, he realised it was Jess. He jumped up and quickly looked in the mirror to check his appearance. His skin was pale and he had brown spiky hair. He wore big black boots, black skinny ripped jeans, a black sabbath band t shirt and a blue denim jacket adorned with patches and pins of all his favourite bands.

He ran down the stairs taking two steps at a time. As he reached the bottom of the stairs the smell of Christmas hit him. A concoction of smells from Turkey to cinnamon and also what he was sure was a sniff of Brussel Sprouts! Harry could hear his mum in the kitchen. As he began to open the door he shouted 'I'm off out with Jess'.

But before he could grab the door handle, he heard his mother shout 'wait a sec'.

Harry turned around to see his mother coming from the kitchen. She was a plump short woman with blond hair that was slowly turning grey. She was wearing an old Christmas jumper her sister had bought her several years ago. It was a barrage of colours; purple, green, yellow and pink, that clearly didn't go together. Thankfully it was mostly covered by the piny she wore.

'Now where'd do you think your going?'

'I'm off out with Jess'

'Don't go out she can stay here'

'No, I want to go out and I don't want to stay in'

'But it's Christmas eve. Your father will be home soon. I thought we could sit down and watch a Christmas Carol. Come on Harry. Its tradition, we always do it and you love that film!'

'I just don't care anymore' Harry replied.

Oh, Ok, well look you go out and have fun then and I'll see you later'

'Ok, bye mum I'll see you later'. Harry quickly kissed her on the cheek and walked out of the door.

As his mother stood their alone, she touched her cheek where he had just kissed her and held it there for a while. She knew when the children grew up and left home things would be different but she was not ready for this Christmas. She wanted her children back. All of them sitting around the table. She wanted that feeling of fullness when she saw them opening their presents. Yes, they were adults. But to her they were the most important thing in the world. And she needed them. At least for one more Christmas.

'Just place one foot in front of the other, it's not that hard'

'Oh, isn't it?! Well usually when I do that there isn't a chance that I'll break my neck'

Harry burst out laughing.

'It's not funny!' Jess exclaimed.

'Just let go of the side and I promise you won't fall. I will hold your hands the whole way around'

'Promise?'

'Promise'

Jess still hesitated though. Why did she agree to go ice skating? She had no-coordination at all. She looked up at Harry who was smiling and encouraging her but she continued to grip the side of the rink as hard as she could. Oh, what she wouldn't give to just be having a hot chocolate and a donut on the other side of this icy death trap, watching other morons who go ice skating only once a year fall on their backside and hobble off the rink because they tried to do something that people were not engineered to do.

Harry still trying to get Jess to move realised that he needed to be more persuasive so decided to take a direct approach.

'Ok I'm getting you to do this now'.

'No Harry don't' She replied.

But before she could tighten her grip once more, Harry had grabbed both of her hands and led her away from the edge. Her legs wobbled, spread and jigged in protest but eventually they and Jess's heart rate calmed down. She was actually doing it. She was actually ice skating. She looked around at all the lights at this park and all the people in the rink but then it all faded away when she looked at Harry. She smiled at him and he smiled back. In that moment she realised something. Something that she had never told Harry or even anyone else before but she knew she had to blurt it out. She couldn't control it any longer.

'Harry I lo-'

BANG!

Jess Slipped on the ice, lunging herself forward onto Harry who fell backwards hard, hitting his head as he fell. Harry now looked at Jess who lay on top of him. His back was aching, his head was pulsating from the bump and he could feel his bum was about to drop off from being frozen to the ice. But as he looked at her he finished her words for her and whispered 'I love you too'.

Chapter 3

Drip, drip, drip. Santa stood their becoming more and more impatient.

'Oh, come on' he pleaded.

A few more drips came but not the desired response. A loud knock came from the door and Paul the head elf shouted from the other side 'Come on big man it's time to go!'

'Baubles and mistletoe, stop interrupting me today Paul, I'm trying to pee!' He shouted back.

'I'm sorry Santa but the portal for you to leave the North pole closes in 5 minutes. You have to keep to schedule!'

The toilet door swings open and Santa comes out. He is now in his full outfit hat and all.

'Zip' Paul chirps.

Santa does up the zip to his trousers and they both make their way to the reindeer barn.

'Did you really have to leave it this late to pee?' Paul moans.

'Hey look I just needed to make sure I left it as late as possible before I leave. Do you realise just how many glasses of milk I have to drink and cookies I have to eat? My bladder is not what it used to be I'm not five hundred and eighty anymore you know'

Yeah I guess it is a lot to drink'

It is. Oh, look can you tone down the big guy jokes a bit'

'Well Santa with all due respect....'

'I know, I know I've been a little bloated these past few years but all those milk and cookies add up'

Paul paused for a second 'Well have you ever considered not eating millions of cookies in one night'

Santa was stopped in his tracks stone dead and looked at Paul horrified. A lone elf from maintenance who was nearby dropped his candy cane and stood their frozen to the core. Santa felt lost for words, he had never heard such disregard. He took a few deep breaths and tried to compose himself.

'Paul. I have to eat the cookies and drink the milk. It's the most important part of my job'.

Paul began to reply 'Well it's not the most impor-'

Santa quickly interrupted 'No Paul it is the most important part. More important than the presents. You seen when I take a bite of that cookie and sip that milk the children know I have been. Yes, they may never see me but it's that which keeps their Christmas spirit and belief in me alive. Anyone can give someone a present, but only Santa can take the milk and cookies.'

'I'm sorry Santa I never realised. Sometimes I get so wrapped up in making sure everything is running properly I forget what it's all about'. The pair of them continued to walk, passing the maintenance elf who was trying to pick up the remains of his smashed candy cane.

*

As they opened the barn door Santa was greeted by his reindeers and sleigh. This sight on Christmas eve, still even now gave him goosebumps. His reindeers stood their majestically, tall and proud and as he ran his hand over the sleigh, he took a moment just to take it all in again once more. This old thing had seen some sights and been in many close calls. From the time a Kangaroo had jumped in the back while he delivered a skateboard to Charlie (9) in the Australian outback, to the time he had to take a hard left to narrowly miss a plane flying over the Atlantic Ocean. This sleigh had so many new parts over the years, some would argue it wasn't the same sleigh but Santa knew it was.

As Santa looked out at the stary night sky through the open barn doors he could see the portal glistening away. It's beautiful array of colours lit up the sky but its purpose went far beyond that, for this portal was the only way in or out of the North Pole. Once out of the North Pole there was no way of getting back in and it was undetectable to all who ventured near. The only way to get back in was through the portal which would open for 10 seconds as the light of Christmas day arose.

'So, can you give me a status report on the reindeer. How are we looking for tonight's run? Santa asked.

'Well I made sure they were all fed and watered, but there are a few things to run by you just to make sure everything goes as smoothly as possible'

This isn't my first time in a sleigh you know'

Paul looked at Santa sternly 'Being prepared and knowing the correct maintenance for your reindeer and sleigh can never be something you know too much of'.

Paul and Santa both passed for a second and then he continued.

'Ok firstly Rudolph at the front is doing good but his nose has been going dim a little. I've used the nose glower 3000 spray on him today so he should be fine for the whole trip. If he isn't though there is some under the seat. Dasher has had no problems and neither have Dancer or Prancer. Vixen however has been getting a little snappy lately so just be careful he doesn't bite you. Comet, as you know, his front left knee has continued to play him up ever since you hit that billboard in Texas'

Hey that billboard came out of nowhere' Santa protested.

'Yes, it magically appeared' Paul sarcastically said before continuing.

'Well Comet's knee and Cupids' hip are causes for concern still. I've had Clement the vet look over them and he has worked on them all year but it's not getting better'. Therefore, to make sure they see it through take a break in Panama, Russia and Kenya. Finally, Donner has been doing great as well as Blitzen although there both being really excitable so just watch they don't burn out of energy to quickly ok'.

'Great thanks for all the info' Santa said as he got in the sleigh.

He felt the reigns in his hands and held them tight, ready to fire up the sleigh and start the long night ahead.

'Better get going, the portal closes in 2 minutes' Paul said.

Santa simply nodded and looked out to the night sky. He raised his arms.

'Wait!' A voice shouts.

Bursting through the side barn door Mrs. Claus comes through. Paul curses 'damn and candy canes' at this further pressure on the deadline.

'You weren't really going to go and deliver Christmas presents without saying goodbye first, was you?' She questioned.

Santa smiled and jumped out of the sleigh, he grabbed both of her arms and looked into her eyes.

'You were sleeping and you looked so peaceful, I didn't want to wake you' he replied.

'You never go without saying goodbye' she insisted.

He smiled back at her and simply said ok. As he looked at her he felt the same way now that he had all those years ago when they first met. Back then he was simply delivering as many gifts and doing as many good deeds as he could. Travelling as far and wide as he could, but with nothing other than his legs. The legends surrounding him had already began even all those hundred of years ago, but he didn't do any of it for recognition or to be called a legendary figure or Saint. He simply did what he did to make the world a better place.

Santa had never even planned to meet Mrs Clause. It had happened when he went to her house to secretly drop off some gold for her poor father who would have become destitute without it. As luck would have it whilst the rest of the family were out working the fields when he dropped the money off, she was in the house and caught him in the act. Whilst he did try to get away, she was a strong-willed woman and she sort to understand what he had done, as she had never seen such generosity before.

From this encounter he explained to her his mission and she knew it was something she wanted to be apart of. It was only with her help that he managed to expand his goal and make Christmas what it is now. It was her who found the elves, lost in the wilderness, dwindling in numbers and without purpose and gave them life again. It was her who trained the reindeer and taught them how to fly. And it was even her who found the North Pole when they were searching for a place to call their home.

She truly was a magnificent woman and the only reason he could be who he was. She had come along with him on his life's mission and made it more beautiful, amazing and fulfilling than he could have ever imagined.

Cough, cough 'Sorry to interrupt this lovely moment but you have got all of thirty seconds to get through the portal before you ruin Christmas' Paul anxiously pointed out.

Santa raised his eyebrows at both of them 'I better get a move on then'.

Santa once again got back in the sleigh and grabbed hold of the reigns. He gripped them tightly and loudly shouted out at the reindeer. 'On Rudolph, on Dasher, on Prancer, on Vixen, on Comet, on Cupid, on Dancer, on Donner, on Blitzen'.

Santa slapped the reigns and the reindeer shot in to action and the sleigh flew out of the barn at lightening speed. Mrs Clause and Paul looked on as they watched Santa head into the night sky. As he drew close to the portal, he exclaimed loudly for both them and all the elves to hear.

'Merry Christmas to all and to all and goodnight'.

As Santa went through the hole and vanished Mrs Clause and Paul stood in the now empty barn for a second.

'Ever the showman' Mrs Clause proclaimed.

 'I wish he would be a more timely one, my heart can't take much more of his escapades'

'You get used to it'.

'When?'

'After a thousand years or so'

'I look forward to it'

'Well come on let's go in and have some coco and wait for jolly old Nick to return'.

Chapter 4

'I'm just going to look at it. Let me just look' Jess pleaded.

'No, you are not' Harry defiantly responded.

'I promise I wont touch it'

'I don't believe you'

Jess playfully punched Harry in the arm and he acted hurt as they both laughed 'I'm your girlfriend and you won't let me check the back of your head to see if there is a lump. You could have a concussion or be bleeding'

'Well it hurts'

'You are such a baby. Your supposed to be a tough metalhead who goes to gigs and gets into mosh pits throwing yourself around with no care for your personal safety. Now be a grown up and let me look at your little boo boo'

Harry gave up 'fine, but no touching'

'No touching got it' Jess repeated.

Harry tentatively moved his head so Jess could inspect the back of his head. He looked towards the rink they had just been skating on and focused on a mum and dad holding their little girl's hand as she tried to get to grips with the ice. It reminded himself of that age. The first time he had gone onto the ice rink he had felt so scared and gripped both of his parent's hands so tight, but his dad wanted him to start skating on his own. Harry didn't agree with that plan. That plan felt like a one-way ticket to Falling Overville and he wasn't ready to board that train. His dad though undeterred got down on one knee and said to him 'It doesn't matter if you fall down, or even if it hurts, because you can always get back up again'. As Harry pondered on that memory, he felt a sudden jolt of pain on the back of his head.

'Ouch' he yelped out.

'Sorry but I had to touch it, good news though there is no lump their and it isn't bleeding, so you probably won't die' Jess rebutted trying to justify touching it.

'Well I'm glad for your expert medical opinion' he quipped back.

'You are very welcome'.

They both paused for a second and just smiled at each other.

'So, what do you want to do now?'

'Well Harry in my expert opinion I would recommend after any bump to the head that you be prescribed hot chocolate with marshmallows and a donut'

Harry thought about this advice for a second.

'Ok I shall take that medicine Dr.Jess'

He grabbed her hand and they both stood up. He leaned into her as if to kiss her but instead whispered in her ear.

'You're paying'

*

Jess was now standing at the coffee van placing their order with Harry stood beside her. The blends of smells just oozed delight as coffee, hot chocolate and roasting nut aromas danced into their senses.

'Hi can I get two hot chocolates with marshmallows please and can I also get 1 sugar donut and' at this point Jess looked at Harry as if to check he was sure and he simply nodded back.

'And also 1 jam filled donut with strawberry frosting and sprinkles'.

The vendor took a few moments and then gave Jess the drinks and donuts. Harry took a look at his donut and his eyes beamed with glee as he then bit into it. He moaned with pleasure at all its sugary goodness.

'Very manly. How is your pink donut?'

'Absolutely fabulous. Hey make jokes all you like but tasty has no gender and this bad boy is tasty' Harry declared as he finished off the donut by licking the remains off his fingers.

The pair continued to walk along and admire the park, the hot chocolate and donuts now resting heavily on their stomachs. They decided to play ring toss on one of the carnival games but both failed miserably. As they licked their wounds, they saw a small mini rollercoaster and decided to have a go. For Harry though that was a big mistake as the mixture of hot chocolate, jam filled pink donuts and a bump to the head all became accelerated by this child's ride which to Harry was going the speed of light. Harry just about managed to unbuckle himself and ran down the exit ramp, before hurtling the previously delicious treats back up into the nearest bin. As Harry remained half bent over the bin and Jess rubbed his back, she saw the most fantastic sign hanging over one of the many wooden huts 'win 2 tickets to Lapland- raffle prize draw inside'.

'Shut the front door' she shouted.

Harry slowly pulled himself up straight, still a little dazed 'What? What is it?'

'It's 2 tickets to Lapland in a raffle!'

'What?'

'Lapland! You know where Santa, the reindeer and the elves are. Oh my god I have always wanted to go. Come on we are buying so many raffle tickets' Jess declared as she pulled Harry towards the wooden hut'.

*

'You know you are ceritifiably mental?'

'I call it certifiably genius'

You spent £10 on raffle tickets'

'Harry, it's called playing the odds, the more tickets I have the better my odds of winning' Jess reasoned.

Harry knew when a battle with Jess for her to see common sense was lost. As the pair of them sat in their pod on this Ferris wheel Harry looked over their hometown.

'Why do you want to go Lapland so bad anyway. Is it because you want to see Santa and tell him what you want for Christmas? Harry joked.

Jess nervously laughed back 'Of course not! Shut up!' she exclaimed.

'Oh, my days you really do don't you'

'No!'

'You actually believe Santa is real, don't you?'

Jess went to protest her denial further but gave up and retorted back 'Look I just don't think we should rule it out. That's all I am saying'.

'Santa Clause'

'Yes'

'Jolly old Saint Nick'

'If you prefer'

'Jess your 17. He isn't real. Santa is not the man who sits for several hours a day down at the shopping centre for 4 weeks a year'.

'Look I'm not stupid I know that, but you never know, the one in Lapland could be real and even if he isn't, he's the closest I'll get to the real Santa. And at least their it's like being in a constant Christmas wonderland with real reindeer'.

Harry was still clearly baffled by what he had heard.

'Ok I get the winter wonderland and I get real reindeer and I get the whole it all feels magical but Santa'?

'I know it's crazy but I choose to believe that there is a possibility that Santa is real, however slim that chance is.'

'Slim is being optimistic'

'True but Santa is, or at least was a real person'

'Nope'

It's true. There was once a Saint Nicholas who would roam Europe secretly delivery gifts to people in need. He would help people however he could and its even rumoured he's brought some back to life. So, whose to say that if he could do that, he couldn't keep himself alive'.

Harry sat there in stunned silence and while he thought Jess's belief was completely bonkers, he couldn't believe how much she knew so he asker her 'How do you know so much?'

'Joys of being a goth type of girl, I guess. Not many people want to be friends with you and hear your whacky theories, so I ended up spending all my time in the library and I love Christmas so much, so I just read up about the history of it'.

Harry smiled at her 'Well I enjoy every minute with you' he leant into kiss her but she ducked out of the way, so hard in fact that their pod on the Ferris wheel jolted.

'Whoa hold your horses their I'm not getting anywhere near your mouth after you've been sick' Jess declared.

Harry slumped back into his seat and this time looked down at the winter wonderland below.

'Beautiful isn't it?' Jess said.

'I guess so'

'Don't you just love Christmas'

'Um not really' Harry muttered.

'What! You don't love Christmas?'

'No not anymore. Its good for kids I guess but it means nothing to me anymore'

'Is that really how you feel?'

'Yeah, why?'

Jess got up from her side of the pod and sat next to Harry and hugged him as if to protect him. Harry loved to hold Jess but this felt weird to him, whilst still nestled in he enquired 'what's this for?'

'I just think it's sad' she softly replied.

'That I don't like Christmas. Its not that big of a deal'

'Yeah it is. Everyone should have something to hold on to, something that is pure and that they love deeply. Something that is childlike still you know'

Harry said nothing for a few moments while he thought about what Jess had said. He understood what she meant but the love for Christmas was gone. He did still like his heavy metal though. And that made him feel just like what she said. He loved it. It transported him to child levels of happiness. Those moments where for just a small amount of time he could truly clear his mind and forget everything.

'You know that's how I feel about music'.

'Is it?'

'Yeah it is. You know I'm not totally devoid of feelings.'

'I know you're not'.

They both sat there for a few moments in silence. Harry might have loved Jess but he didn't know how to do deep conversations.

'Well at least your dream of going to Lapland involves a real place' Harry said breaking the silence.

'What d'you mean?'

'Well where I want to go doesn't even exist or at least not yet'

'Where is that then?'

'Well if I ever have millions of pounds, I'm building this idea. It's heavy metal island'

'Heavy metal island?'

'Yep, heavy metal island'

'Wouldn't going to a few rock festivals be easier and cheaper?'.

'Yes, it would but this would be outstanding. It would be a place that all metal heads could go too. A full island dedicated to nothing but metal and all the genres with in it. Run for and by metalheads and it would be on a tropical island. Somewhere you wouldn't be shivering in your tent while rain leaked through'

'It sounds great'

'Oh, it is. And all the best acts from all around the world would come in every week to play. And there would be days and weeks dedicated for all types of fans, from thrash metal to punk to nu metal and classic rock.'

'You have really thought this through haven't you' Jess realised.

'Oh yeah of course, also all the drinks are named after different bands'

'Oooo he's still going' Jess whispered to herself.

'A place like that see. A place like that would be my dream destination. It's just a shame I'll have to become super rich for that to happen' Harry shrugged.

'So not for a while then is it?'

They both laughed.

'No, it might be a while. Although maybe it's for the best if it's not me. If I decide what acts are playing then everyone else might get sick of me booking slipknot and Metallica to play back to back for 4 hours a day every day'.

'It might get a bit tiresome. Although that might be the case for playing heavy metal everyday in general' Jess queried.

Harry had a half mocking, half serious look on his face. Jess took one look at Harry and knew she was in for a lecture.

'Heavy metal every day would never be tiring. There are so many varieties. So, it could be different all the time to encourage people to come'.

'So, what is your dream line up then for your island? What's the dream acts for a week?

'Dead and Alive?' Harry queried.

'No, you idiot, alive only, we might all be metal heads but we cannot go resurrecting Jimi Hendrix'.

Harry sat their and started to think about his dream line up for a week. Jess did the same too and they began to come up with their perfect line up, whilst overlooking their hometown, and while Harry may not have cared anymore about Christmas, he did wish this Christmas eve would last forever.

Chapter 5

With the perfect Christmas eve over Jess lay in her bed. As she looked at her clock the time struck midnight so she grabbed her phone and messaged Harry 'Merry Christmas. I love you and I can't wait till we are on metal island together'.

Buzz, Buzz. Harry's phone vibrated and lit up. He was close to sleep but not quite there. His eyes heavy he felt around for his phone on the side board. He read the message and smiled. She always did this, sending messages as soon as she could, after dates, as soon as it was midnight on birthdays, anniversaries, whatever it was. He replied back 'Heavy metal island forever. I love you too'

As both fell asleep, full of love and dreams, across the world Santa was on a mission. He stood atop a glorious palace and breathed heavily. As he stretched his calf's in preparation before flying down the chimney, he looked at Dancer who shot him a disproving look.

'Don't look at me like that, it's only right I do this'

Dancer snorted.

'Oh yeah, I could leave it but the list is the list and he made the list'

Dancer snorted once more.

'Thank you. I appreciate it. Now you remember, if I am not out in 10 minutes fly back to the North Pole. Got it'.

Dancer snorted and nodded. Santa looked out over the city's night sky, took a deep breath and the jumped down the chimney. Now inside the palace he could see just how grand it was. The room he was currently in was all red and gold quite like his sleigh. It was as large as the entrance to a mansion. Massive drapes adorned all the windows. The fire place behind him was large and roared, lighting up most of the room in a hazy glow. There were many portraits of different people, all very formal covering every inch of the walls and there were sofas dotted around the whole room but none face each other.

Now inside the palace Santa decided he wanted to act fast. This was not something that he particularly wanted to hang around for, but lists were lists and since Mrs Clause and Paul had helped him devise them over four hundred years ago, Santa had not failed in delivering presents or coal once.

Santa threw his sack on the floor and started to rummage through looking for the lump of coal. As he got his hands on the coal, he could hear two voices coming from down the hallway and he froze. He wasn't ready to go back up the chimney, so with sack in one hand and coal in the other he quickly ducked behind him one of the sofas. The voices grew louder and louder until they walked straight past Santa and through to the next room. Santa stood up and breathed a heavy sigh of relief, glad of the passing of the guards.

He walked up to the fire place and placed the coal on the floor, but as he did so the whole room lit up. The two guards looked at Santa and Santa looked at them. He couldn't go up the chimney it would go against Section 3 of The Saints Code to not use any powers in front of others but he had to do something, anything, something, think.

Santa ran as fast as he could out of the room and down the corridor. The guards ran after him trying to shoot at him and screaming at him to stop and surrender. Bullets flew through the air and pinged off ornaments and walls narrowly missing him. With the sound of gunfire and the guards shouting, more guards were alerted and gave chase. Santa kept ducking and diving down corridors as much as he could, but the guards were closing in, shutting off his exits from every angle. There was no way out. No escape. This was it. The shouting began to intensify but just as all hope was gone, he saw a window at the end of the corridor. This was no ordinary window though, this was a stained-glass window showing the portrait of Saint Christopher, the patron saint of travellers. Here to save him in his moment of need on his journey.

Santa began to run again, as fast as his over one thousand-year-old plus legs could, and as he bounded down the corridor, he loudly whistled three times and at the sound of the third whistle, clattering and bells chiming could be heard from above. As he grew closer and closer to the window Santa braced himself, stretching his arms out in front of him he leaped ten feet into the air and smashed through the glass window into the cold night. As he flew out of the window the reindeers were flying across his path and caught him, but just barely as he flew over the top of the sleigh and only just managed to prevent certain death by grabbing the runner underneath.

As the sleigh jolted and bounced aggressively Santa's grip loosened and one hand slipped off the sleigh's runners. His arm was screaming in pain now but he pulled himself up with all his might and landed in the sleigh. Still breathless he tugged on the reigns and the sleigh sped off into the cold night with another name crossed off the list.

*

Back in the North Pole Paul was in the control room with two other elves reviewing the Sleighdar. Mrs Clause walked in and saw him working through calculations.

'Everything ok?' she asked.

Paul carried on working through the calculations as he replied.

'Not really, Santa is massively behind schedule and based on these calculations, with all of Europe still to deliver to he is going to be cutting it extremely fine to be back in time before the portal closes and we cannot allow that to happen.'

'Like every year then'

'It's closer than ever though, but I don't know what to do'

'You can only control what you can control Paul. Why don't you go get some sleep? When did you last rest?'

'Um, probably 5 weeks ago now, So I'm fine'

'No, you are not, you need to sleep'

'I will once he's back'

'He's just entering Europe now Paul' Darren and Tracey declared simultaneously.

'Both of them can hold down the fort for his return and I will stay up too, isn't that right guys?'

Darren and Tracey both turned around at the same time and nodded. They were usually a part of the stuffing department, but since they got married in 1813, they volunteered every year to help Paul track Santa's movement by the several Sleighdar's in front of them, although with Darren's glasses being as thick as milk bottles the accuracy of where Santa was exactly could be dubious at times. Paul decided not to protest any further, he was tired after all and there was much work to start tomorrow in preparation for next year.

'Okay, okay I shall retire for the night'

'Good' Mrs Clause replied.

'But if anything comes up at all you come get me straight away. Promise.'

'Yes, I promise. But look nothing is going to go wrong.'

As those lasts few words came out of her mouth the whole room went completely dark. A massive gust of wind began to blast through the control room as if a hurricane had suddenly erupted from nowhere. The wind continued to rip through the room and a constant loud growling noise could be heard over the blasting wind. This continued for all of thirty seconds and then suddenly as it had started, the darkness lifted, the wind stopped and the growling ceased.

In complete shock Mrs Clause and Paul were both laying on the floor, but seemingly unharmed.

'Are you ok?' Paul asked.

'I'm fine, you?' Mrs Clause replied.

'I think so, what the hell was that?'

'I have no idea'

As both of them looked at each other perplexed a piercing scream filled the room, almost primal it ripped through Ms Clause and Pauls hearts. They both turned around and saw Tracey alone holding Darren's glasses. There was no trace of him except for his thick spectacles. Both jumped up and went to comfort Tracey as she cried uncontrollably. Paul at this point noticed the control panel. It was completely and utterly destroyed. The Sleighdar's were all cracked and broken. The wires at the back were all had all been pulled out and ripped apart too. There was now no way to see where Santa was. If he got lost there was no way of finding him.

Paul was absolutely petrified. What was going on? He decided to check the box. He left Mrs. Clause comforting Tracey and ducked behind the control panel. It was a complete mess. He began searching frantically throwing pieces of broken panel and wiring over the top of the control panel.

'What are you looking for?' Mrs Clause asked.

'A phone' He shouted back.

'A phone?'

'Yes, a phone'

'We don't have a phone. There has never been a phone at the North Pole.'

'Yes, there has' Paul slowed himself down and composed himself. He looked at Mrs. Clause who still holding Tracey was completely baffled.'

'There has been a phone in this control room since 1939'. He confessed.

'Why and how did I never know?' She shouted back.

'In 1939 Santa was delivering presents in Germany. As the sleigh flew low over Berlin a stray bullet from the war raging below broke through the bottom of the sleigh and shot him in the leg. It hit one of the main arteries in his leg and he was very lucky not to bleed to death. He was losing consciousness and couldn't control the sleigh any longer. On the outskirts of Germany in the countryside he crashed the sleigh into a barn. It was only through sheer luck that it woke up a Jewish farmer not yet caught by the war. The farmer took him in, managed to remove the bullet and save his life Santa managed to get back through the portal with just 0.3 seconds to spare. The next day he built two phones, one for the sleigh and one for the control room but with the precise instruction that it was only ever to be used in a life or death situation. I call this one of those times'

Paul continued to look for the phone which should have been locked behind the panel but the sheer debris was proving difficult to search through.

'Why didn't he tell me?' Mrs Clause asked.

'Because you'd want him to stop. Naturally you would if you had known he was that close to death. Over a thousand years he has served the world, bringing Christmas joy. He deserves a break but he can't, he won't let Christmas end'.

Paul managed to get to the back of the panel but the safe in which the phone was held in was open and the phone was missing. Paul stood up, he couldn't look Mrs Clause in the eye. The colour had drained from his face and he felt light headed, there was absolutely no way of contacting Santa. He went to tell her but before the words came out of his mouth, gut wrenching screams could be heard from outside the control room. At first it was one elf, then two, then three, then more and more screams could be heard coming from al around the North Pole. The sounds engulfed Paul, he felt like he wanted to be swallowed up. He went over to the intercom on the wall and pressed the button that connected to speakers all around the North Pole and called out 'All personnel I repeat all personnel please make your way to North Pole square immediately'.

*

As Paul and Mrs Clause stood in the North Pole square all the personnel started gathering. They were mostly elves but others were employed here too taking sanctuary from the outside world. There were polar bears who helped with heavy loads, Unicorns that helped create the blend of magic dust to fuel the reindeers to fly, the goblins who worked in gold craft and the trolls who were expert tool makers.

As all of them slowly came into the square Paul started to see it was not just Darren who had gone missing, the horrifying reality was clear for him to see, everyone who had a partner was missing them. Their soulmates had gone.

With the crowd gathered around him Paul tried to find out what had happened but all the stories were exactly the same throughout the whole North Pole. The darkness had taken over, the wind was powerful and the growling could be heard. Paul was utterly lost, he didn't know what to do, he looked at Mrs Clause but it seemed neither did she. The elves began to shout out in desperation 'What happened to my Jeremy? Where's Amy? Where's Adam? Where's Doris?' The noise kept getting louder and louder, they began asking where Santa was, what these two were going to do. The noise became deafening.

'Silence everyone!!' Mrs Clause bellowed.

The whole square went silent, you could hear the sound of a pin drop.

'We must not panic here. As it stands the details of what has happened here as of yet are not clear. All we know is all our loved ones are missing. At this point it would be unwise to presume any further as to whereabouts with wild speculation'

'Where is Santa?' A voice from the back shouted.

Mrs Clause took a moment to compose herself 'During the darkness the Sleighdar and all methods of communication have been destroyed. We have no way of contacting Santa, however you all know he is extremely capable and I have no doubt that on his return he will be able to help us find out what has happened here tonight. In the meantime, I must ask you all immediately to return to your accommodation and initiate protocol zero. Do not leave your accommodation, barricade all windows and doors and please most importantly cease using any electrical equipment and don't use any magical devices or conduct it. Paul and I will contact you via the speaker system with further updates as soon as we can work out what to do next'.

The elves, unicorns, polar bears, trolls and goblins all began to disperse. Paul and Mrs Clause continued to stand in the middle of the North Pole square. Thrust into being the joint leaders and unsure of what to do next. Paul talked but in barely more than a whisper.

'I've never seen this happen before, what do we do?'

'I don't know, but I think I know who it is'.

Chapter 6

Santa was stood outside of his sleigh and began to sing a song to the tune of silent night.

'Silent night, holy night

Guitars are cool, drums are alright

Round your bass solo, ride the lightening

My guitar skills are so frightening

I really want some coco now

I really want some coco now'

As Santa pulled his sack out from the back of the sleigh Blitzen gave him a dirty look.

'Not appreciating my fine voice are we' He quipped.

All the reindeers shook their heads in unison. Santa however rather liked his twist on the classic story and continued to hum it to himself. He looked up at the isolated snow-covered house that lay on top of this hill and pulled out the list of residents; Dad-John, Mum-Linda, Son-Harry.

As Santa put the list away, he felt the ground underneath him begin to shake violently, the wind howled through, throwing him against the sleigh and everything went to complete darkness. Sana was scared, he knew who this was. It was Crnobog the god of darkness and the ruler of the world of the dead.

Santa mustered all his power deep in his soul and managed to unleash the light from inside him. The darkness and light battled with each other, entangled, the light tried to attack the dark from every angle but it kept shrinking further and further until Santa bellowed 'ENOUGH!'

At that moment the complete darkness stopped and the night sky returned. Santa looked around but he couldn't see his attacker, for Crnobog was a completely dark figure and blended into the night's surrounding.

Santa shouted out 'I know you are there Crnobog, show yourself you coward'.

A loud growl deafened Santa, piercing his ear drums and then the force of the wind was channelled, lifting Santa up in the air, before throwing him into the ground with such ferociousness it was as if Crnobog wanted to send Santa straight to Hell.

At this point Harry awoke, hearing the noises from outside he turned on a light and ran to his bedroom window. He watched what was happening below and couldn't believe the evidence of his own eyes. Santa was in front of him but he seemed to be battling with a black figure. The figure moved as if like a gas, not human, not fully solid. Santa was flung against a nearby tree and was clearly losing as he struggled to pull himself back up. There was some light coming from his chest but it was whimpering out he and couldn't battle against the darkness. The reindeers were clawing and pulling to try and get away but Crnobog's power was holding them down.

Harry shut the window and turned the light off and just stood in the lonely darkness of his bedroom for a moment, completely in shock. Jess was right. Santa was real, but what was going on. Harry couldn't comprehend it, his heart was beating out of his chest, he was breathing heavily and despite the sub-zero temperatures he began to sweat. He didn't know what to do. He had just seen Santa Clause. Santa Clause was real. Santa Clause was also in trouble. He knew he had to help, so he ran downstairs and to the front door, he fumbled with the lock, his hands sweaty, he was struggling to get the key in the door. Finally, he managed it and swung the door open, he ran out towards Santa but at that moment the black fog over Santa changed. It now became something that resembled human, actually he was human, or at least looked like one.

The figure was almost pitch black, his chest was the width of three men and his shoulders were like boulders. He was over 10-foot-tall and now fully formed he was a menacing beast of a figure. Harry froze. He then began to slowly turn his head towards Harry forgetting about Santa like he was a toy to discard. Harry was scared now; he was absolutely petrified and frozen to the spot. The figure's head and body were now fully turned towards him. Behind him Santa tried to stand and shouted as best as he could.

'Harry run!'

But before Harry could move at all Crnobog flicked his spade like hands and sent Harry flying backwards through the air and towards the entrance of his front door. Crnobog then spoke, his voice seemed to implant itself in Harry's brain. It was cold, heavy and piercing all at the same time.

'Do you dare interfere with me? You are weak and worthless. I almost pity you. You must suffer for interrupting my work. I will take from your soul everything you care about'.

Crnobog opened his palm and out shot a Jet-black stream. It pierced Harry's chest and he withered in pain. He could feel love and hope draining out of him, he tried to cling on to his thoughts in order to block out the evil. His mum, his dad, his brother and his sister. Christmas's all together, running around the house which was full of decorations and smells, all of it carried on sweeping away. He could feel it coming for Jess, he tried to fight it as he screamed in agony but he was powerless. He tried holding on to the memory of Jess. The first time they ever went to a gig together, it was a local band in a backstreet bar whose name he couldn't remember, but he would forever treasure the memory because as the chorus played that was the first time, he kissed her. He kept trying, holding on to the memory so tight, till it hurt and burnt him, but he could feel the love and memory being torn apart into a million pieces. The tears poured down his face at the agony of it all.

Santa, now barely conscious somehow puled himself up to his feet. He tried to harness all the power he could, all the goodness from simple deeds that created pure magic. He threw both of his hands together and pointed them towards Crnobog and roared from the depths of his soul.

The light that shot out was blinding. It was so bright it lit up the night sky back to day light. It hit Crnobog who released his grip on Harry who then fell to the floor in a slump. Crnobog withered in pain for a few moments but he managed to regain control and shot back with the darkness. It hit the light of Santa and both of their essences shot into the sky, covering them and the house in a dome which was swirling blackness, nothing could be seen outside of it but it was light inside of the dome.

Both Santa and Crnobog locked eyes at each other, neither was prepared to give up the fight. As it raged on the earth began to move underneath so violently it rocked the foundations of everything inside the dome. The tree behind them uprooted from the ground, the windows of the house all smashed simultaneously and its very foundations started to come away. Then in the middle of them a hole began to appear. It grew larger and larger until it was almost 20 foot wide. The hole itself began to scream and started to hiss. Still stuck in the middle of all of this, the reindeers were pulling and pushing all they could to get away, but Crnobog maintained through his wind control a full grip on them, preventing them from going.

With the hole growing even further Rudolph's front hooves were scrambling to stay away from the hole. Rudolph tried everything but then the front two hooves were in the hole, Santa hearing the noises of his reindeer looked towards them and Rudolph stared back at Santa, the red nose was so bright it looked like it was about to pop, but Rudolph's eyes clearly showed terror. The hole seemed to become brighter and an orange glow began to appear from its depths.

Santa knew he didn't have much longer he could feel the darkness winning. He dropped to one knee briefly, as he felt the power of the darkness take hold. He managed to get back up to two feet once more now and fought back.

His eyes closed he thought of all that mattered to him. What was in his heart and his soul, it was only this, the power of love, of hope, of caring and giving that could win against this. He thought back, he went to the day he first met Mrs Clause and to the first time he ever gave a gift when he was just a young boy.

It began to work, the light was winning, cracks of light appeared in the dome above. The light went over halfway towards Crnobog, then three quarters, until it was nearly touching his chest. As it edged closer and closer Crnobog looked down at it and then up at Santa and for the first time his stone cold faced turned to desperation, Santa was going to win. He would not let this happen.

Bang! The struggle stopped, but it wasn't light but rather darkness that was now everywhere again. The dome now broken, Santa lay on the floor barely alive, Harry was unconscious on the step of his own front door and the Reindeer's were all teetering over the edge of the hole, their efforts to continue to move from their invisible trap were hopeless but they still continued to try and free themselves.

Crnobog surveyed the scene he had just created and laughed. He began to move towards Santa slowly, with no urgency at all, for he knew that he had beaten him, he had conquered Santa Clause. Now standing above Santa he rested a foot on his chest. Santa could barely move and put up no resistance. His eyes filled with tears as he looked up hopelessly at Crnobog who began to speak, but this time more slowly and almost softly.

'Don't cry. Your tears are pointless'.

Santa tried to push Crnobog's foot off his chest but he couldn't make it budge as he stood their grinning.

'Yes, squirm Santa, squirm. Horrible isn't it? Feeling completely hopeless, knowing you have no control. Well that's how I have felt for over a thousand years! Ever since you banished me to the underworld, but I waited and got more powerful. You aren't better than me any longer. Your love and light wont win. I can assure you that. Darkness will reign supreme now and forever'.

Santa could barely breathe but he managed to get out a few words through gritted teeth 'You won't get away with this. Christmas and hope, it's more than me'.

'Is that so? Well I already have got away with it. Nobody can stop me now'.

'The elves and the people they'

'They what? Fight back? Hold hands and sing songs. My god you are so naïve. Did you not think I would have learnt from the last time you stopped me? There won't be any elves to help you. I've taken them, but not just all of them, I have taken half of them, separating them from their soulmates'.

Santa's eyes widened.

'Yes, yes that's what I want to see, that fear in your eyes. See I remember all that time ago when you told me about how they all had soulmates and how they would slowly perish without them. I know all your weaknesses. And all these people you trust, spouting about the human spirit to love, they are fickle. Once you miss Christmas, they'll forget you ever existed.'

'It doesn't matter about me. I'm not important, but the people their spirit will survive'.

Crnobog dug his oversized foot into Santa's chest even further, moving closer to his neck as Santa gasped for air.

'You know what old Saint Nicholas I wanted to finally end your immortality tonight, but I'll give you a fate worse than death. I'm going to let you live just so you see how truly wrong you are. And once it's destroyed you, when you are begging for me to put you out of your misery because you can't stand to watch your beloved human race turn on itself any longer. Then, then I will bring you to the underworld. Then you will see what you put me through and I will make you watch your broken humans even more as they become nothing. Just like you are.'

Crnobog finally let go of Santa's neck, as he looked down at Santa, he knew he had won. Crnobog walked over to the reindeers. Heading straight to Rudolph Crnobog stroked the struggling reindeer. As he did so the brown fur turned to black and Rudolph's eyes turned to red. He slowly walked around each of the reindeer, almost methodically, turning their fur black and eyes red.

Once all the reindeers had been turned, Crnobog made his way over to the sleigh. Smiling he looked at Santa, still spent and laying on the floor unable to move. He began to talk to Santa softly, in a way that was as if he was talking to a friend about his hopes and dreams.

'I always wanted to ride the sleigh' he began, as he caressed the sleighs engraving.

'It's just an amazing thing isn't it, how it's magical, how it works with the reindeers. Oh, the reindeers. Such fantastic creatures. They will come very useful.'

Crnobog got into the sleigh and grabbed hold of the reigns. As he looked back at Santa one last time, he could see Santa was beaten, he said nothing. He then looked forwards and snapped at the reigns. The reindeers lurched forward and down to the hole to hell. As the sleigh went out of site, the hole it had just gone down disappeared and everything around it in an instant defaulted back to normal. The usual night sky returned, the house was back on its foundations, its windows untouched and the pulled-out tree looked completely normal.

Santa lay looking up at the sky for hours unable to move, he tried to take every last star in he could see, inspecting each one individually, looking at its place amongst the others around it. In all his years he had never done that. As he began to feel his body able to move again, he tried to move his right foot. The pain was excruciating as he lifted it just off the ground but it fell straight back down. He then moved his left leg and tried to throw it over his right. With all his might he lifted his leg and threw it over but the resulting pain was so hard to bare and he screamed into the snow.

Over the next hour Santa slowly but surely pulled himself up limb by limb, inch by inch until he was up to a standing position. He could feel every bone in his body was at breaking point and his muscles were crying out in pain but he stood tall.

The daylight was starting to take over from the night, Santa knew he didn't have much time. He saw Harry's slumped body in his front door step and hobbled over to him step by step. As he got to him, he could see that at least he was still breathing. Santa couldn't leave him here to be found. He bent over and picked Harry up, usually this would be nothing to him but at this moment the pain set his body on fire and it took everything within him not to cry out in pain.

Santa began to walk with him, through the threshold of the front door, in to the house, up the stairs and in to his bedroom. As he got in to the bedroom, he collapsed forward throwing Harry on to the bed as he laid across him. Santa didn't want to move but he knew he had to get going, he hugged Harry as tight as he could and slowly got to his feet.

The room he was in was surrounded with rock and heavy metal band posters and memorabilia. Harry and Santa carried the same essence in their love of music. That's why Santa had the made an electric guitar for him. He knew Harry wanted to start a band but that he couldn't afford the guitar. It all seemed futile now but Santa had thought if he could get one not so much a child anymore to go from a non-believer to a believer again, through the essence of music that was also part of Santa's soul, then that would spread Christmas spirit to Harry and beyond.

Now as Santa looked down at Harry, all he hoped was that there was something of Harry's soul left. Crnobog's attack lasted so long and there was no way of knowing, as of this moment, what affect that was going to have on Harry or indeed the world. Crnobog had destroyed Christmas and an innocent soul. Santa knew it was bad but he had no idea how to solve it. Crnobog was not just playing at mischief and dabbling with dark magic, now he had declared rule for darkness to take over, for love and joy to be swept from the world.

Santa stood there as a single tear came down his face.

'I'm sorry'

He turned around and walked out of the room, down the stairs and out of the house. Dragging his broken body, he walked over the hill at the back of the house. He had no idea how to navigate his way home right now. He had no sleigh and no reindeer but he had to keep moving forward.

As his feet trudged through the snow, he knew he had to find a way to get back home. Back to the North Pole. He thought about what await him there. Was Crnobog just trying to scare him or had he really taken all the elves soulmates? Was Mrs Clause safe or even alive? He had to believe she was. He had to believe that even without Christmas people's spirit would shine through. But right now, all he knew was that as he walked in the daylight of Christmas morning, belief was all he had.

Chapter 7

364 days later

The embers cracked and popped as the fire raged, it was the only thing here with any fight left. Santa sat on an old big red chair next to the fireplace, alone. He was so close the heat was uncomfortable but he just didn't care, he hadn't moved from this chair in 3 days, or left the room in a week. He sat in front of the fire place with just his red trousers and a white vest on. His beard was unkept and his top was stained. He didn't see the point in making any effort anymore, what was the point in doing anything? Everything he had worked towards and all that he had accomplished, it all meant nothing now.

Crnobog had foretold everything perfectly, people had begun to turn on each other out there. In some ways it was on a large scale, with wars breaking out all over the world as the want for peace died but it also was on a much more personal level too. It was people's individual relationships that began to fall apart. There was no love between people any more, caring had disappeared and passion was not just a distant memory anymore but had been completely forgotten. Partners, parents, siblings and friends. All those connections, the bonds forged through happy memories, shared experiences and tears, all of that meant nothing to anyone now. Sometimes people came together but for nothing more than practicality. There was

7 Billion people in the world and every last one of them was truly alone.

The situation at the North Pole was just as grim. With half of the elves gone and all the remaining losing their soul mates, things had quickly escalated. It had taken Santa several months to get back to the North Pole. He had to stow away on a flight, swim through frozen lakes and walk thousands upon thousands of miles to get back home and when he finally managed to get here, the site that greeted him had shook him to his core.

Some of the elves had gone mad, unable to cope with the unknowing and separation from their loves ones they burned their accommodation to he ground before disappearing into the wilderness, unable or not wanting to be found. Santa didn't know if they died out their or had found isolation. The ones that had remained faired no better. Greif stricken they slowly succumbed to death by broken heart. For while humans could struggle but overall, usually coped with the loss of a loved one, the elves couldn't cope. This was because the shared experiences and memories they had with their soul mates faded and disappeared leaving only the pain to remain. That mixed with no sense of purpose with Christmas no more, they simply broke. By the time Santa had got back thousands had gone and in the following months he watched on hopelessly with the unicorns, polar bears, trolls and goblins by his side as he held the hand of every elf that fell in their last moments.

Santa continued to stare at the fire place. He would give everything just to go down one more. To deliver a present.

But all good things must come to an end he guessed and clearly Christmas wasn't meant to last forever and neither was he. He was reminded of this as he looked down at his hands. This last year had aged him for the first time in a very, very long time and as he looked at those hands all he could think was that they were the hands of an old man. They looked frail and worn. Yes, he had looked old for an eternity now, but he had always felt full of life and energy. Maybe it was just mental, but now all he felt was tired.

The door to the room opened with a creak and Mrs Clause walked in. Saying nothing she walked over to the other chair perched next to the fire and sat down. Santa didn't look up at her or even acknowledge that she had come into the room. They both just shared the silence together, watching as the fire continued to glow. After several minutes Santa finally spoke.

'Do you remember when we first found Rudolph?'

Mrs Clause looked at Santa, she said nothing but just gave a soft knowing look with her eyes.

'I can still remember it now. Shunned by the rest of the reindeer he was. I couldn't believe it, here this reindeer was with a gift so precious and yet he was unloved by his own because he was different. A little bit of me never forgave the other reindeer for that'

'They were all young too and they did accept him eventually' Mrs Clause countered.

'I know, I know. But there were days back then when I thought It was impossible to train him. He lacked so much confidence. Three years it was you know, three before I could get him to fly on his own, five before he could with the rest of the reindeer. That bright red nose of his, that gift saved my life on many a foggy night and I'd tell him that every time but Rudolph still hated it. Still felt like an outsider. I just hope he knew just how much love I had for him'.

'We all did and I know he knows that'

'That image of him, that fear in his eyes. I really hope there isn't anything left of him now, because if there is, he would just be so scared' Santa croaked a little but he held back any tears.

Mrs Clause held his hand saying nothing. She knew that there weren't any words she could say to bring any comfort, so she did what she always did. Just reminded him she was there and held his hand. As she did so she could feel his hand had aged, it felt almost leathery and as she glanced at them her eyes gave her the proof that her heart already knew, her beloved husband was starting to grow old. He hadn't said anything to her but she had known for a while now, but she couldn't be angry with him for saying nothing, for she was aging too. It hadn't begun to really show on her face physically yet but inside she could feel herself aging. Her strength was going and her bones ached in ways they never had before.

Mrs Clause sat in silence and thought to herself about what Crnobog had told Santa about how love would go from the world and how that had become a reality. When Santa told her that she sort comfort in her knowledge of her inner strength and her love for him. She knew that could never happen to them. But while she sat their holding his hand in silence, she realised they were starting to slip away too. They had given up, they were hiding from each other, they weren't a unit anymore. They may have still sort comfort from each other but was that really the same thing as love she wondered. All she did know was for the first time, her unshakeable belief had begun to crack.

*

'You know for a so called beautiful magical creature you don't half crap a lot!'

Paul looked at the unicorn who shook its head, snorted and then pointed its head towards another unicorn at the back of the wooden barn.

'Ok Karl, so your saying Hayley is responsible for all the unicorn dung, is that right?

Karl the unicorn nodded enthusiastically but Hayley shook her head aggressively in defiance, refusing to take the blame.

'Well who ever it is you have out done yourself'. Paul declared as he bent down shovel in hand and picked up another batch of hay and unicorn mess.

He carried on for another 10 minutes until all the mess had been cleared. Tired and worn out Paul sat on a bale of hay and got out a flask. He undone the lid and poured himself a cup of hot coco. As he drank it, he could feel it working to warm him up. He sat there in the barn for several minutes watching the unicorns. They ran between each other playing games and teased each other pulling on their horns. Sometimes this could involuntarily cause a shot of what resembled rainbow to come out from there. When this happened, it would escalate into a free for all between them to shoot the rainbow-like substance at each other, which when it hit them made the unicorns tingle like they were being tickled.

Paul found a small amount of comfort in that, for it was this rainbow-like substance that was used as the raw material for the reindeer's fuel to fly. How exactly it worked Paul had no idea. All that he knew was that between the unicorns, the chief elf scientist Ryan, a number of trolls and the cooking department, reindeer fuel was made. While it wasn't being used to make the reindeers fly anymore, at least it was still providing joy here, in a world where that had perished.

Paul drank the rest of his coco and put the lid back on his flask. He couldn't stay here and whimsically reminisce much longer, he had work to do and plenty of it. He still had to tend to the polar bears, check the trolls were doing ok and the goblins well he let the goblins look after themselves, they didn't like being disturbed without a good reason as GRA GRA once told him before shutting the door on his face.

As he walked back through North Pole square, he was reminded of the events that took place here a year ago and how all those faces that had looked to him for hope, how all of them had since gone. Paul shook his head, trying to shift the images out. He decided to replace them with happy ones like playing ice hockey in the square. They were always huge games, with way too many players on each side and crowds of onlookers, all of whom should have been working but had caught Paul at a weak moment.

As he walked, he saw out of the corner of his eye a large stick as big as him and a broken bauble. He smiled to himself. He grabbed the stick and began to dribble the bauble along, sweeping back and forth he began acting like he was playing hockey and for a moment he was with everyone, cheering him on, as he started to commentate his own gameplay.

'Paul sweeps to the left, now quickly to the right, now back to the left, now back to the right, now back to the left, he moves forward, now to the right, to the left, he shoots...... And it's in'

Paul cheered to himself and lifted the stick above his head in celebration as the bauble now completely destroyed found its final resting place on the bottom of the workshop steps. As Paul brought himself back to his senses, he could hear faint noises coming from the workshop and he realised she must have been in their again.

He walked up the steps and through the large front door in to the workshop. He had to take a moment to compose himself. He hadn't come in here for a few weeks now as it was just too painful and the whole room would just fill him with sadness. This was a place where millions of children's dreams had come true every year, where toys they had hoped for all year got made, were put in Santa's sack and magically appeared under their tree every morning. It wasn't just about Santa, every single one of these elves had made each of those dreams come true.

Now the workshop lay empty of souls. The tinsel was still on the pillars and the tree still took centre stage in the middle of the workshop but it all felt hollow. Toys stood half assembled on production lines with no homes to go to. Paul had thought about moving some of the toys and clearing the workshop but he couldn't bring himself to do it. Deep down he hoped that one day production could start again. That the elves would magically appear again and begin making toys and that this nightmare would be over. But while that hope was still with him, he knew that it was false, and he had accepted that things would never be the same.

Over in stuffing he could hear noises being made and he saw a dim light shine from the corner. Paul went over and saw Tracey in the stuffing department working on an oversized cuddly bear with big eyes and a real bow tie finished with a golden bell. She was sitting there, her glasses on the bridge of her nose, as she delicately smoothed out the stuffing, making sure it fit into every last part of the bear. Behind her over one hundred and fifty completed bears sat on display.

'Hey Tracey' Paul whispered.

'Hiya Paul, you ok?' She replied softly.

'Yeah fine. Have you been in here long?'

'Just the last three hours, got another two of these done' she said as she held up the bear.

'Great, you've been doing well making all these bears, haven't you?'

'Thank you. I can't believe I used to be able to do fifty an hour. Sometimes we would go in a race wouldn't we Darren'. Tracey looked to her side and then remembered that Darren was gone. She slumped back into her chair but looked at Paul and smiled.

'So, what are you doing in here? Checking to see if I'm still being productive is it? She joked.

'No, no, I was just sorting the unicorns out and heard someone was in here so thought I'd better check it out'

'Well it's not going to be the big man is it?'

'It doesn't seem so'

'I don't think I've seen him now in over a month. I think he's avoiding me'

'He's avoiding everyone, you, me, even Mrs Clause'.

'I just hope in this time of isolation that he takes, that he finds a way to reverse all of this'.

'Tracey, I don't know if he......'

Tracey put her hand up and shushed him.

'Paul, hope is all we have now to hold on to. It's that alone that keeps us going when there is no light'.

Paul said nothing, he understood what Tracey said and shared that belief despite his own pessimism. He decided to help Tracey, so he pulled up a stool next to her, grabbed an empty bear and began stuffing it.

They both carried out this exercise in silence for over an hour. Paul had to admit to himself he always thought this job was boring and mundane but he felt something quite therapeutic in the process and seeing the end result of the full oversized teddy bears. Eventually though he broke the silence.

'Tracey, can I ask you something?' he asked.

'Go ahead'

'I know it's a delicate thing to ask and it might sound blunt, but, but'

'But what?'

'How are you still alive when all the rest have gone?'

'Your right that is blunt'

'Sorry'

'I don't know for certain but one of the things that I can do that others couldn't is remember the good times. All those millions of positives working with him every day, I remembered them all. Oh, he did annoy me mind you, with his constant pranks and sarcasm but the greatest gift I ever had was being able to spend every moment with him'

'But doesn't it hurt still? All the other elves would cry out about how losing them hurt'

'You bet your candy canes it hurts. The pain I feel not having him right by my side I can't describe it. But I believe that one day we will be back together, however that may happen and until then I will forever hold him in my heart'.

Paul said nothing for a moment. He just took in all Tracey had said and tried to process it. He just couldn't believe how she remained so strong.

'Well I'm glad you are still here' Paul said in a barely audible voice as he tried to keep his emotions in check.

'Me too' Tracey replied.

After a few moments Tracey hesitated but then decided to ask Paul a question.

'Can I ask Paul. How come you never had a soulmate?

'I don't know. I guess those that decide that for us never intended for me to have one'

'But don't you get lonely? Don't you feel incomplete without someone?'

'Not at all. Just because I didn't have anyone who I loved or who loved me in that way, doesn't mean I have ever felt lonely. I have all of you and that is where I got my love from, those thousands upon thousands of connections. That means everything to me. I've always guessed that I'm just different, I never sort that soulmate out and they never sort me, but I guess that's ok. Especially when I've always had to be in charge of you lot'.

They both laughed, but this shared moment was cut short when the doors to the warehouse were opened and in came a site that both thought they would never see in this room again.

'Santa!'

*

Santa stood in the archway to the workshop with Mrs Clause by his side. Paul and Tracey couldn't believe he was back in here. Since the first day he returned he hadn't been able to bring himself to come into the workshop. Seeing the place without the elves and all the toys flying everywhere it was all too much.

'What are you doing in here?' Paul asked

'Well I am Santa Clause, it wouldn't be right if I didn't make an appearance in the workshop on Christmas eve'

'You ok Santa?' Tracey enquired.

'Fantastic, I got my darling wife and the two best friends that anyone could ask for by my side'

Santa gave a massive smile and looked between the three of them but as he looked back to Tracey, she could see it in Mrs Clause's eyes that this was all an act. For Santa deep down, couldn't think of anything worse than being in here, a place that once filled him with such joy, now filled him with dread. He was only here because Mrs Clause had dragged him out of that room, she couldn't stand to watch him waste away in front of that fire like he was and she knew that tonight was going to be tough, so if even for a moment she could get him to not think about it and just remember who he is, it was worth it.

'That's quite the collection of teddy bears you have their Tracey' Mrs Clause pointed out.

'Thanks. It has kept me busy that's for sure'.

Everyone then just stood there in silence, they had no idea what to say to each other. As the moments continued to pass the tension grew as none of them spoke. They all begged for someone to speak while the silence grew deafening but there was no end in site until finally Santa blurted out 'You know I always wanted to make the teddy bears real'.

'Make them real?' They all replied.

'Yeah you see sometimes children can be so lonely and they can feel like they got no friends, I thought brining the teddies to life, it could solve that, so they always felt they had someone to turn too'

'That's such a sweet thought' Tracey replied.

'It's because of little things like that, where you thought of all those ways to make the children happy, it's because of those reasons I love you so much'. Mrs Clause hugged his arm as they shared a moment.

Paul however broke this sweet moment 'that is the stupidest thing I have ever heard!'

'What!' They all shouted back.

'Real life teddy bear, it's an idiotic thing to do'

'Why?' Santa shouted.

'Because you want to give consciousness to an object. What level of consciousness are you going to give them? Will it be like a dog level of consciousness or a human? And if you give it that then your opening yourself up to a whole other world of problems. What will you do when it develops its own feelings? Or has aspirations and hopes and dreams? What will you do if a teddy bear gets arrested? You know what Santa I really don't think you thought this one through.'

'Yeah I guess I didn't' Santa said as he took in the barrage of questions from Paul.

A moment passed and then they both looked at each other and laughed hysterically. They continued to laugh at the exchange they had just had and the absurdity of it. How Paul had just got so angry at this illogical idea of Santa's and also how Santa had only realised in that moment just how flawed his idea really was. Together they laughed until they were reduced to tears.

'I've missed your outbursts Paul' Santa chuckled

'Thanks. I would say I had missed your whacky ideas like that but I'd be lying, you know they frustrate me' He replied laughing as he spoke.

'You know what I miss? Mrs Clause said as they both turned around to look at her and Tracey.

'I miss the jamming sessions'

Santa shut his eyes for a moment and remembered them.

'They were so good'

'Not so much when they were on Christmas eve' Paul remined them.

Santa chuckled 'They were the best, because I know they wound you up so much and you know just how much I enjoy doing that'.

'Yeah it is great feeling like I was going to have a heart attack every Christmas eve because you would leave it too late to leave, or the presents wouldn't be right or I'd fear you'd lose the reindeer on your deliveries. Yeah those were great moments for me.'

The whole room fell silent, it took a few moments for Paul to catch up and realise what he had said.

'Santa I'm sorry I didn't mean that it was your fault that they…….'

'You know what we should all have a jamming session right now' Mrs Clause declared.

Both Santa and Paul looked unsure, but then Tracey enthusiastically agreed 'Yes, let's do it'.

Mrs Clause walked out of the stuffing section of the workshop and after a few minutes passed her voice could be heard in the distance.

'Oi you lot, come here'

They all obliged and walked out in to the centre of the workshop. What greeted them was a spectacular site that

Santa hadn't seen in what had began to feel like an eternity. Four electric guitars, four amps and four microphones with stands. They all walked up to them, taking their positions and feeling the guitars. It felt so special just to hear the basic strumming of fingers against string and they were all aware of just how important this was. As while music was still remembered here outside the North Pole it had been completely forgotten.

It seemed when Crnobog had attacked Harry his loss of what made his soul had spread across the world. And as it was defined by music that was what the world had lost. It wasn't just that it stopped being made either, it had been completely forgotten about and erased like it never existed. Bands never came together, operas were never performed, raps never battled, pianos never played, rifts were never heard, the list of tragedy was endless but quite simply the world didn't have music. And the world was a soulless place without it. But just for this moment they all collectively decided to block that out and enjoy what they could, hear and now.

'What shall we play?' Tracey asked.

'I think some rock classics would be a wise choice' Tracey offered.

The rest of them nodded and they began to play tune after tune for hours and hours of the best songs they knew, from Stairway to Heaven by Led Zeppelin and Go Your Own Way by Fleetwood Mac, all the way to AC/DC's Thunderstruck and Metallica's Whom the Bell Tolls. They played the lot. As the last note of the last song played, they could feel the soreness in their fingers and their voices were raspy from singing along to every song. But despite this they all felt the best they had in a vey long time.

As they all stood their spent, they looked at each other, proud of their session and nodded to each other with Santa then enquiring 'Encore anyone?' They all emphatically shouted no and Santa faked outrage for a second despite his tired state.

Suddenly the large fire place at the end of the workshop lit up with a whooshing noise. The four of them were taken aback. The fire place was six foot- tall and fifteen-foot-wide and it hadn't lit up in over a year. For it only ever lit up on its own accord. Because this was no ordinary fireplace but rather a magical one. They all ran over to it and looked on as the flames glowed across their faces.

'Is this anything to do with you Paul?' Santa asked.

'No, I promise it isn't'

Santa turned to Mrs Clause 'This isn't you is it? I know I've been down but don't get my hopes up with things like this'

Mrs Clause pleaded her innocence 'No I swear it isn't me either'.

'Could it be him?' Tracey whispered.

The thought crossed his mind, yes, he was cruel and taunting but Crnobog had won and he knew it. Besides he hadn't contacted him since, why would he do it now? The fire seemed to grow and then it crackled and popped and out spat a white envelope which headed straight at Santa, hitting him in the belly before he caught it with his hands. As he looked at the envelope which was singed on the sides he trembled in disbelief, it was a letter to Santa.

Chapter 8

Beyond the North Pole borders there was no songs being sung. There was nothing but misery and loneliness in the world, and for Harry he had become so numb. As he lay in his bedroom, he was completely lost in life now, he had no purpose or direction. He couldn't even remember music anymore, there was just this void left in him, an empty hole where magic had once been. The worst part of that though was that while he couldn't remember music, he could feel something had gone, that he had lost something important, but with no idea what that was it just left him feeling broken inside.

Harry knew thing had changed in the world in the last year. But he didn't really know what. The world was angrier sure, he could see that, but that had been happening for years. He'd also broken up with Jess at the beginning of the year. She hadn't done anything wrong, he just had no feelings towards her or anyone else for that matter. He couldn't see the benefit of being with her, there was no economic or practical sense to it like his parent's relationship. Harry remembered in that moment how she took that news. She had seemed really upset and shocked by it, she kept screaming at him that it didn't make sense and shouting off about love and that she loved him and why didn't he love her. Then finally the last thing she said to him was, do you love me? And he had said No. She had ran away crying and he never saw her again.

He felt bad about that at the time but looking back now he really didn't understand her reaction, he had only been truthful, he had no idea what love was. How could he say he felt that? It wasn't his fault that she got upset about that.

Harry decided to stop day dreaming and go get some dinner from downstairs. As he got into the living room his mum and dad were both watching tv.

'Hey Mum we got any food?' Harry asked.

'Get yourself one of those microwave meals from the freezer, oh and don't think I haven't noticed you haven't paid your rent money yet. I want it tomorrow. No excuses.' She spoke cold and matter of fact like.

Harry was just about to go into the kitchen when he saw the next news item and it stopped him in his tracks. There were videos of people with signs from all around the world protesting. The signs all had different things on them but as the images flashed on the screen, he could just about make out some such as 'Where is the Love?' 'Peace not War?' And 'Santa is Real'. As he saw that last sign an image shot through his mind. A distorted face. A ray of blackness. And he heard himself scream, in his own head. The imagery threw him for a second and sent a shiver down his spine. He'd had these weird images in his dreams but he had put it down to an overactive imagination, this was the first time he had ever had them when awake.

'What are they on about their dad, Santa is real?'

'A load of nonsense boy that's what it is. No good lots spouting crap that they make up when they should be out working. See look at them all, kids with no life experience and a few older people who've never done a day's work in their life. Too much time on their hands see. Santa is real. Never heard of him. But I bet if he was real, he'd come give that lot a slap or two!' His dad had basically forgot Harry was even there by the end of that rant.

Harry could see his dad's fist was clenched as he continued to watch the news. He watched it every night without fail but it made him so very angry. Harry decided to go in to the kitchen to sort his food out and leave his dad to calm down. He saw no point in this anger. To be honest with himself he saw no point with any emotions that people shared. They were useless, it slowed people down, making people less efficient. They really had no place in the world as far as he was concerned and those weirdos on the television were not something to worry about. They were interesting to watch but that was as far as it was.

As Harry peeled back the film of the microwave lasagne, he looked at all the rolling hills behind the house all blanket covered in white snow. He moaned to himself, he hated this weather, it would make driving to the office a real pain tomorrow, but he knew he would have to go in, regardless of the weather. For tomorrow 25th December was a special day. He had been working at his office job for

6 months now ever since dropping out of school and it was his review period. If he passed, he knew he was secure in his job and he could get a raise and that would be the best December 25th he could ever ask for he thought.

His dad shouted from the front room 'Hey these nutters keep shouting love over and over again now'.

At this moment Harry heard a sound like the world had just fallen down and as he braced himself, he could see a massive red hole in the kitchen floor, which was becoming louder and louder and making growling noises. His lack of feelings was gone now and he felt fear like he had never done before. What was this? There was a massive hole in the floor and it was going to suck him in, his heart was going a million miles an hour, he couldn't breathe, he kept on walking back, trying to escape but fixed on this hole, his head hit an open cupboard door.

'Ouch' He yelped out.

He looked down at the kitchen floor and it was normal once again. This was so weird, Harry was seeing things, he was definitely tired and needed to go to bed.

'You ok in there? Why you making so much noise?' His mum shouted.

'Yeah I'm fine, just hit my head on the cupboard'. He replied.

Harry slowly walked towards where the hole had once been. He stuck his foot out and tapped on the tiles with his tip toes. It was solid and secure. He breathed a big sigh of relief.

'Not about to die then' Harry muttered to himself.

He put the microwave meal in and turned it on. As he watched it bubble, he hoped for a much more normal tomorrow than these tired hallucinations.

'Let's not have any more portals to hell tomorrow' he whispered to himself.

The microwave pinged.

*

Down below the surface Crnobog sat on his throne and gazed over his underworld kingdom. He had built himself his own paradise in the year that had passed. The elves he had stolen from Santa now satisfied his every need. He made them break rocks, he made them dance in chains for his own amusement, he would even get the elves to go above ground and hunt for food and if they tried to escape or mount any sort of comeback, he would torture them by throwing them into the pool of lava that lay bedside his throne. As being in the underworld meant they couldn't die or even get injured, he could still make them work after drowning them in the lava, but the jolly part to him, was they felt every bit of pain while they were thrown in and those screams were so satisfying to him and they kept everyone very compliant.

Along with the elves he also had the reindeer at his disposal. He looked at them in the corner of his molten rock lair and grinned to himself. Compared to how Santa has last seen them they were unrecognisable now. They were still black just how Crnobog had changed them, but now any hint of themselves behind their bright red eyes was gone, being here had all but destroyed them. They were still good to fly but they had been reduced, to barely skin and bone and most of their thick hairy coats had fallen out from the stress and of dealing with the heat that comes with being chained up, unable to move next to a lava pit.

He would love Santa to see this, to see what his loyal magical creatures had become. What being Santa's elves and reindeers had done to them all.

The funny thing was though, Santa was already a broken man. He had watched Santa's hope and will fade as he had returned to the North Pole. Watching those moments, oh they were pure joy to him. In those first few months as Crnobog watched on, making sure not to reveal himself, he was worried Santa would figure out the way to save Christmas and destroy him but he never did.

The holding of his nerve proved fruitful. He watched as the man who had destroyed him and banished him to the underworld fell to pieces. Santa was seeing the world tear itself to pieces. Rejecting love, while forgetting Christmas and music. Crnobog was rejoiced. If he celebrated Christmas, he mused that he would see it as all his Christmas's wishes coming true at one.

A year later now and Crnobog's dream was complete. Sure, there was a handful of people across the world who still remembered love and Christmas protesting about it, but the whole world had brandished them as outcasts. These people couldn't feel love or even remember what Christmas spirit truly was, they had just somehow retained these words. But with absolutely nobody left truly feeling these things or remembering them properly Crnobog felt safe in the knowledge that his work was now complete.

Crnobog got up at this moment from his throne, all the elves that were near gasped and froze wondering what he was about to do next. As he walked past them all, he felt full of glee as he saw the fear in their eyes. He decided to do nothing to any of them today. The fear to them was as bad as the act itself so he was just happy to keep them in suspense.

He moved towards the reindeer. They all backed themselves into a corner but chained and with nowhere to go it was pointless. Crnobog looked at Rudolph at the front of the pack and walked up the line of the reindeers who all flinched as he passed. As Crnobog stretched out his hand Rudolph tried to pull away, but he just stroked the top of the head and bonked the nose. Rudolph's nose was now black and didn't shine. The unique reindeer with a bright red shiny nose, Santa's favourite Crnobog thought, was now just as pathetic as the rest. And that too made him very happy.

The master of the underworld decided that with a year passing since the battle with Santa and all his dreams coming true. he wanted to celebrate the occasion as best as he could. He wanted to observe his work first hand and go above ground to watch these puny people tear each other apart and become machines. As he looked at the reindeer and then at the sleigh, he decided in that moment what better way to do that than in the sleigh on Christmas eve.

Crnobog snapped his fingers at one of the elves who came towards him tentatively.

Frustrated he shouted 'Come here now!'

The elf picked up the pace as best as they could.

They spoke nervously 'How, how can I help?'

'Tie the reindeer reigns up for me and connect them to the sleigh' He ordered.

'But, but sir, if you wish to take the reindeer out with the sleigh they might die. They've had no magic fuel for so long, the flying will exhaust them and it could kill them'.

'Are you disrespecting me elf!?' He bellowed.

'No sir, no sir, I promise' The elf shouted fearing for their life.

'Then you should remember that I am your god and you should address me as such' Crnobog screamed at the elf and then in his anger he grabbed the elf by the throat and threw them into the lava. As the elf screamed in pain the others all looked on petrified, locked on to Crnobog wating for what might happen next.

'Would anybody else here like to tell me what to do?' He shouted out to complete silence.

He pointed at 2 elves 'You two, get on with sorting this sleigh out'.

The two elves quickly obliged in order to escape any similar treatment and worked quickly on the sleigh and within moments they were done. Fear does really work as an effective motivation tool Crnobog thought to himself.

He got into the sleigh and steadied himself, holding the reigns in his hands. He was still so glad he had managed to take this from Santa and now he would use it on the same night that he would and to go around the globe just like he would. But the greatest thing of all was he was going around the world to survey the misery he had created and for him that was the greatest gift of all. He snapped the reigns and the reindeers came to life. He kept snapping as they flew higher and higher out of the underworld, leaving the elves alone below he bellowed out 'Ho, ho, ho, Merry Christmas'.

*

Jess sat on the floor by her fireplace and looked out of the window towards Harry's house which sat atop of the snow-covered hill. She avoided him to make sure not to see him for fear of further heartbreak but she still missed him deeply every day. Nearly a year on since they broke up and she still couldn't get over it. The whole thing made no sense to her in the slightest. They had been in love, deep love. She had felt it in her soul and she knew he had felt it too. To just say he never felt that, it wasn't just a lie, it was like a totally different person had told her that.

But Harry wasn't the only person that Jess had felt change, it was as if the whole world had. Everyone from friends to family, to total strangers. It was like overnight everyone had stopped loving each other. By the middle of January her parents had broken up. A marriage over after twenty-five years, with no warning. Jess was devastated by it, but neither of her parents seemed to care. They acted to each other like complete strangers who had never met. He dad moved out soon after and Jess's mum became a zombie. She barely spoke to her and when she did it was only to get something from Jess. The mother she knew was gone and was replaced with this cold unloving shell.

Between this and Harry, Jess had hoped she could find some comfort in her friends but they all had given her the cold shoulder as well. The whole friendship group had blown itself apart. They argued and even physically fought each other. The whole lot of them seemed to become bitter enemies and this anger and all their sense of reasoning only worsened as time went on. It seemed that any care that the group had once had for each other was now long gone.

With all this hate in the world Jess hung on to the one thing that everyone else had seemed to forgotten. The ability to love and care. With these philosophies in mind Jess had still tried to be herself despite this crazy year. She gave change to the homeless, she held doors for people, she smiled at them even if they looked back at her confused, she did everything she could to put positivity out in the world and with the sea of negativity surrounding her she constantly wondered if it was all worth it. Being like this and fighting against the world to be kind was exhausting. People would be angry at her for being kind and caring to others, for understanding their plights and misfortunes. All this did though was reinforce to Jess just how much this world had changed but that she knew that regardless of that she wouldn't and couldn't be stopped. For Jess knew that deep inside that even if her positivity wasn't making things better, she knew she wasn't making things worse and contributing further negativity to a world that was now so cold.

Jess turned on the television and was met with the news showing videos around the world of people protesting with signs such as 'Where is the love?' She had heard of these people before and had read up about them online. They were a group who believed that we used to live in a different world than the one we were now in. That an event had happened around a year ago that broke the structure of reality as we knew it.

The groups ideas were illogical and highly flawed in many ways but they believed in the concept of love. They confessed they didn't know what it was but they knew it affected how the world previously acted. As well as this they believed there was a magical immortal being called Santa. But once again their knowledge about him was no better. All they did know was that a few of the leaders of the group had remembered his name and believed he was a central figure in their ideology. They believed Santa could restore everything so that this universe would seize to exist. Jess hoped that were true. She hated how the world was now. Whether at home with her mum or at school surrounded by hundreds of other people all Jess felt was truly alone.

With all these thoughts racing through her mind, she felt like she was about to explode and she didn't know what to do. She couldn't vent these feelings to anyone. They would all think she was crazy for feeling different to them. Besides her mum was out so she was home alone. Then suddenly she had an idea. She was going to write a letter. That way she could get it all out. She could express how she truly felt without fear of judgement and then she would keep the letter to herself. It was just for her. Maybe to put away in a box, never to be seen again, or to get out when she wanted reminding of how she felt right now in this moment if she began to start acting like everyone else.

Jess ran upstairs into her bedroom and grabbed a pen, some paper and an envelope. Stationery in hand she came back down and settled herself in front of the fire. Her heart was racing and her breathing was shallow but this wasn't because of the run upstairs, she actually felt nervous. She felt like she was about to spill all her secrets out. Everything she had kept bottled up for the past year. All her hopes and desires and fears. She began to tear up thinking about it, everyone just over a year ago would say they needed someone to say all these things to, but now nobody did and they didn't want to hear Jess say them either, but now she could release it all even if it was in a letter.

As Jess sat their pen in hand she didn't know where to start or what to say in the letter. She also felt a bit stupid now. She was going to send a letter to herself. How silly was that? Jess decided she was going to push on though and ignore the heckler in her head. Although she took one piece of the hecklers advice and decided to write the letter out to someone other than herself.

Dear Santa

I don't really know why I am writing this or what I want out of it. I just feel that I need you. I know you are probably not even real but when I hear those people on the news say your name, I feel this pull to you inside me.

I'm struggling so much now, the whole world that I once knew is gone and I don't know if it's ever coming back but I know I can't carry on in this one much longer Santa. It just hurts. I feel I'm not truly me anymore no matter how much I try and I don't fit into this new world. This world is too cold. Everyone feels nothing but I feel like I feel everything that they are supposed to be feeling. Like all the emotions in the world that people should have is inside of me. I just want to explode with it, it's too much.

I know that love exists in this world Santa. All I wish for, is that it would come back. I'm not saying things would be perfect, they weren't a year ago. But I know that I always used to feel no matter how bad things were, whatever I'd done or whatever had happened or however much I cried, I knew I was loved.

But now with that gone it just feels like nothing but the darkness. I believe in a thing called love, even if nobody else does. I just want to hold my family again; I want to hang out and chat with my friends and I want to kiss Harry. I need him back so much; I miss all those moments when I felt like everything else in the world faded away. Oh my god I know I am sounding cliché and cheesy now but that's just how I felt.

With Harry now though there seems to be big important moments from our relationship I just can't remember. Sometimes when I think of him, I hum and tap things but people think I'm a freak when I do it. I've never seen anybody else do that so maybe they are right, but it makes me feel so close to him so I do it alone. I'm sure that tapping and humming is what is keeping me sane. It feels like a release from reality.

Writing this letter is stupid I know but hey, the only person who knows about it is me, so hey future me you are an idiot, past me you are an even bigger idiot. You need to wise up, stop crying now, you have had your little vent to someone who doesn't exist so start controlling what you can, but on the other hand Santa if you are real, I need you right now, the whole world needs you. Please come save us, whoever you are and whatever you can do. We need love again in the world and I need some help to bring it back.

From Jess

Jess put the pen down and breathed a heavy sigh. It felt good to get all of these thoughts off her chest. She had been holding on to them for so long it was like a weight had been lifted. She then read the letter back to herself and laughed at what she realised she was saying. She was basically calling herself a depressed teenage girl and was asking a person who doesn't even exist to come help her save the world and that was the most idiotic untruthful statement she had ever seen and she wrote it. Jess wasn't about to save the world. Nobody was. It was all over. Done. Game over. The life support was unplugged. There was no hope of the world truly changing back to how it was and a single teenage welsh girl was not about to change that but it was nice to day dream she could tough.

Jess put the letter in an envelope and wrote 'To Santa' on it. She held it in her hands for a few moments and thought about its contents. She was glad she wrote it, every word in their needed to be said but what if anyone else saw it? What would happen if her mum found it? Believing in love, addressing letters to Santa, she wouldn't understand it, nobody would. At best she'd be outcast, at worst her mum would have her taken away. She looked at the fire and knew that was her only solution, so that nobody else ever laid their eyes upon it.

Jess hugged the letter tightly, like she was saying goodbye to an old friend, she threw it in the fire and watched as the flames devoured her words. She hoped maybe what she'd said in that letter would ripple out as the smoke fumes went into the atmosphere. She was hoping for many things was Jess and while she tried to do what she could to save the world, that she knew was all she had. Hope.

Chapter 9

'Santa what does it say, what does it say?' They all shouted.

'Its, its, oh my it's a letter to me, a letter to Santa Clause'. He exclaimed, unable to comprehend what he was reading.

'From who?'

'Jess Bevan in Wales'

Paul put on his head elf brain 'Santa can you be more specific there is a lot of Jess Bevan's in Wales'

Santa's mind was scrambling his recall was so quick, it had to be to remember everyone in the world's name but he hadn't had to do it in so long.

'It's uh, Jess Bevan, 14 Glyndwr Crescent'

'What does it say?' They all shouted again.

Santa read the letter out to them all. When he finished it, he looked up at everyone and they were all just as shocked as he was. Nobody said a word for a moment as they all tried to comprehend what Santa had just read out to them.

'What does this mean?' Tracey asked.

Santa looked down at the letter and scanned its contents once more. He mumbled as he tried to find the words.

'It means, well it means, there is someone out there who still believes in Christmas!' He exclaimed.

'But didn't our readings show Christmas spirit was down to nothing?' Tracey retorted.

'The proof is here though, she believes in Christmas and if she still believes maybe just maybe we can harness that and get the Christmas spirit to spread'.

Tracey, Mrs Clause and Santa were ecstatic and began to cheer but Paul took the letter from Santa and began to read it, meticulously scanning over each word. He realised their happiness would be short lived.

'Stop, stop. Santa, I know the letter is addressed to you but that is it. Jess doesn't mention Christmas. You already know about the people who remember your name and have heard of the concept of love. We looked at them, there is nothing they can do to help save the world, they can't feel these things they just remember them. I am so sorry Santa it's just another dead end'. Paul felt terrible saying it but he knew he had to for everyone's sake.

The whole group's faces dropped immediately. They thought that their prayers had been answered only for their hopes to be dashed.

'Hang on a minute'. Mrs Clause grabbed the letter and examined it too.

'Santa you can save the world and she is the hope. Read the letter again. She doesn't just remember the concept of love, she can still feel it despite the rest of the world'.

Santa was silent for a moment he didn't know how to take in all of this information being thrown at him but he gathered his thoughts and tried to explain them to everyone else.

'Ok, so if she believes in love still that is great but if she doesn't believe in Christmas, how can I as Santa Clause bring it back to the world'

Mrs Clause retorted back 'It doesn't matter one bit that she doesn't remember Christmas. Do you remember what you said to me all those years ago when we were first delivering presents? You said it wasn't about the gifts at all. The true meaning of Christmas is the kind deeds and helping people. That's what she is doing. She is spreading love. She has love in her. She has the Christmas spirit.

Santa was getting excited again but he had a sudden thought 'But how do we harness that spirit? She has been trying to spread love and it hasn't worked.'

They all pondered this point for a moment and then Tracey just like the rest grabbed the letter. She flicked her eyes through the text and then pointed at the letter, almost jabbing it enthusiastically as she looked around at all the others.

'There it is, there it is. That is how we do it'.

'What?' The rest said in unison.

'Music!'

'Music?'

Tracey nodded 'Yeah music. In the letter Jess said when she hummed and tapped things it comforted her. She remembers music and she said she thinks of Harry when she does it. Don't you see? It's all connected. The way to spread the love and save the world is through music.'

Santa had to steady himself to take all of this in. He sat down on an old wooden chair and looked up at the group. He took a long deep breath before he spoke, taking time to align his thoughts.

'Ok, I believe it now, I think we can do this. I think we can save Christmas'.

The group cheered.

'But if we are going to do this, it has to be now, it has to be tonight'

The rest of the group looked at Santa in shock.

'Santa that is suicidal' Mrs Clause declared.

Paul chirped in 'We haven't planned for this, think for a moment Santa, we need a tactical strategy. If I draw up some plans, maybe in say a month or so, once we have done a few drills to make sure everything will work, maybe then we ca look at......'

Santa shook his head in defiance.

'It has to be right now, this is the only way. Jess's belief is strong right now but we don't know how long that will last and we cannot afford to miss this opportunity. The world has already lost one Christmas and I will not let it lose another'.

The group nodded, they accepted what Santa had said, it really was now or never.

Have you thought about how you will get Jess to save Christmas through music though Santa? It is not going to be easy.' Paul asked.

'Once we get there, we just need to get her to believe in me. Once we have done that, I'll explain to her about music and then we can get her to work on Harry'.

Tracey piped up 'But Jess has tried that herself and it didn't work'.

Mrs Clause interjected 'Yes, but that was just her expressing her love to him, maybe the music, which was the foundation of their relationship will get through to him?'

Santa followed up 'And with him being the source of all of this, if he believes in Christmas, love and music once more, then that might be just what we need to save the world'.

'Well I need to pack some guitars then if we are going to show them what music is again' Mrs Clause replied.

'No, you won't be' Santa said firmly.

'I beg your pardon? I have stood by you for over a thousand years. We have battled everything shoulder to shoulder, we are nothing when we are not together'.

'Have you all forgotten Crnobog is still out there. This is not just about reuniting two forgotten lovers in to each other's arms again'.

'I am very well aware of that and that is why you need me next to you. Don't you dare try to treat me like a woman who needs protecting after all this time!'

Santa smiled, he looked at her face filled with annoyance towards him, but he thought about their lifetime together and how her strong will was what he loved most about her.

'I wouldn't dream of doing that to you. You are needed here, if this all goes wrong, if something happens to me then Crnobog wont stop. He will come here, he will destroy the North Pole and all its wonders, its powers, all the beings that are here, they will all be gone forever. If that happens then the world will be doomed forever. If you are here you can defend it and just maybe you will be able to save Christmas yourself. That goes for you too Tracey. Paul and I will go. The world can survive without an idiot and a control freak but it can't live without you two. The strongest women I have ever known, full of love and defiance that you will never stop fighting for what you care about'. So, let me go just with Paul, but promise me, if something does happen, the pair of you will never stop'.

They both looked at each other and reached out for each other's hand.

'We promise'.

Paul interrupted this moment 'I just had a thought Santa. How in the name of unicorns are we going to get there? We have no transport.'

'But we do Paul, we have John'

'No, Santa'

'Yes'

'No'

'Yes'

'He is way too old, John hasn't seen action in over two-hundred years' Paul pleaded, hoping Santa would see some sense.

'Paul, John is my most trusted reindeer of all time. He may not have flied for a while but trust me, he will work his magic and get us there'.

'Ok, if you say so'

*

Santa was stood in the open barn looking out over the night sky. This moment felt so unnatural to him, at this point every year he would be finalising checks with all the reindeer and sleigh but now as he looked at the portal in the sky, he knew it would take everything they had to make this one last trip.

Paul walked through the side barn door with a large back pack over his shoulder.

'Ready when you are Santa'.

Santa looked over the backpack that was nearly the size of Paul.

'You got enough in there?' He asked sarcastically.

'An elf needs to be prepared for every situation'

Santa walked over to the stable door at the edge of the barn and looked in to the stable at John. His eyes were as old as time itself and his fur was clearly worn down.

'John, I need you. I know it has been a long time but I need you more than ever before, the world needs you. Do you think you can fly us tonight?'

John looked at Santa but then turned away from him. Santa dropped his head to the floor, he didn't know what to do now, without John's help Christmas couldn't be saved. A few moments past and then Santa could feel a light tapping on his head. He looked up and John was there with his reigns in his mouth, banging them on top of Santa's head.

'Thank you, John' Santa said softly.

He opened the barn door and out John came. He plodded slowly but surely until he was in the middle of the barn looking out towards the night sky. This reindeer might not have been so young anymore but he stood tall and proud, he was ready to do his duty.

Paul noticed the reigns in Santa's hand and felt like he needed to point out the obvious.

'Uh Santa, there isn't any point in the reigns, we don't have a sleigh'

Santa looked at Paul and winked 'Oh yes we do'.

He went over to the far side of the barn and up to a wooden locked door. He searched in his pockets and found a large key that was black but rusty and had a little golden string tied to the end of it. Santa unlocked the door and went inside. After a few moments of groans and bangs, Paul could here something being pulled and then he could see it. Santa had a second sleigh. It was much smaller than the normal one but it was a sleigh none the less. Underneath the cobwebs the red wood was broke up by the golden edges and intrinsic designs across its whole body. It was a beautiful site.

'Santa you have a second sleigh!'

'Very observant Paul' he winked at him.

'But how, why? The other is, well it was fine and this a lot more than just a year old'.

'You remember how hard it was for Rudolph to fly back in the early days, well I built this one myself, so he could pull it himself and feel confident with the sleigh. Back then John was the only reindeer that looked out for Rudolph and he used to watch when I trained him. So, when John couldn't do the Christmas eve's anymore, I couldn't stand the thought of him never flying again, so when the rest of the North Pole is sleeping John and I will slip out and fly for a while from time to time, although it has been a couple of years now hasn't it buddy? You sure you got this?'

John nodded vigorously.

Santa got the reigns and put them on John and attached them to the sleigh. He walked over to one of the open stables and grabbed a bucket. He had to make sure to give John some reindeer flying fuel. As Santa presented the bucket to John, he tucked in quickly and finished it all off in moments. With the bucket empty he looked up at Santa his eyes wide and ready to go and do what he was trained to do.

Santa then got into the sleigh and Paul followed. Santa felt he needed to check with him.

'You sure you are happy to be coming with me now? There is no going back from this.'

Paul was absolutely petrified of what may lay ahead but he nodded, he knew it had to be done.

Santa grabbed the reigns tight and then snapped them. John sprinted off out of the barn and they began to fly in the air. As he rose further and further Santa could feel it was taking every last ounce of the reindeer's strength but he climbed and climbed and then they were through the portal. They were out, out of the North Pole and ready to reclaim Christmas!

Chapter 10

'Woah, woah, slow down, slow down John'

Bang! The sleigh crashed into the snowy ground, bouncing twice before coming to a complete stop. Santa, Paul and John were all rattled from the rough landing but they were all in one piece and considering John had not flown this far in a few hundred years he could be forgiven for being a tad rusty.

Groaning Santa got out of the sleigh and looked at the house in front of him, inside was potentially the person who could save the world and for the first time in his life, he felt nervous. His palms were sweaty and he felt sick and his heart was beating so fast he felt like it was about to jump out of his mouth. It was so strange, he was Santa, the calmest, most laid-back person there ever was, but he knew this was make or break. If this didn't work there really was no hope for Christmas.

Santa then glanced up the hill towards Harry's house and remembered what had happened exactly a year ago. The dark images and the pain he felt that night raced through his mind, just imaging it all made him physically feel like it was happening all over again, but he snapped out of it. He had a job to do.

Paul walked up and stood next to Santa.

'So how are we going to do this?' He asked.

'I guess we just knock on the door and explain ourselves'.

Santa and Paul walked up to the door together and he knocked on the door loudly three times. They waited a few moments but there was no reply. Santa knocked again, but still there was no answer.

'Did you definitely get the right address Paul?'

'Santa please! I haven't ever gotten the address of a child wrong in history, I am certainly not going to start getting that wrong now'.

'Well, where is she?'

'Maybe she's out'

'Are you telling me that we have risked our lives to find the person who might just save the world from going back to the dark ages and she could be out!'

Inside the house Jess peaked through the gap in her living room curtains. Who were these people at her front door? An old man, muscle bound with a great big bushy beard was standing next to someone who at first, she thought was a child but as she got a better look at his face could see he was much older. They were a very odd-looking pair and Jess wanted nothing to do with them. In the last year stranger and stranger people had surfaced and Jess was not about to take a chance on two of them who just so happened to knock on her door when she lived in the middle of nowhere.

Santa knocked for a third, louder and longer but still to no avail.

'Santa we will just have to wait, she will be back eventually'.

'No Paul, we cannot wait, each minute we waste could be the last minute that she holds onto the Christmas spirit'.

Santa stormed back to the sleigh and began to rummage in the rucksack that Paul had brought. After about a minute he shouted out 'Yes' and he turned around, proudly holding up a small golden key to Paul, this was not just any key, this was the Christmas key. He had devised it a good few years ago for the houses that didn't have fire places. This key could open any door in the world.

As Santa walked back to the front door, he explained himself to Paul 'If we get inside now, we can have a look around for clues as to where Jess might be and we can go find her'.

Paul nodded along.

Santa turned the key in the lock and they both looked at each other as the door lock clicked open. They stepped inside the house and closed the door behind them. The living room door to their left was shut so they decided to look in there first. As they opened the door however the living room was not empty but their stood Jess in the middle of it, there hope for the future of the world was in front of them, but in her hand, she held a large rolling pin and Jess wasn't baking cakes, she looked ready to fight.

'Who are you two?' She shouted.

'Jess it is ok, we ....' Santa was quickly interrupted though.

'How do you know my name?' Jess asked nervously as she struggled to maintain looking aggressive with the rolling pin in hand.

'Jess it is me, I am Santa Clause'

'Yeah of course you are and I'm the Queen. You are just one of those weirdos, aren't you? Those ones that follow that group around calling themselves Santa so that vulnerable people start worshipping you. Well that is not going to wash with me mister'

Santa was lost on what to say, this was going to be tougher than he thought.

'Jess I swear to you it is me, I am Santa, Paul here is my elf and I have a reindeer outside'.

'What's an elf? What's a reindeer? Look old man you want to prove your some mystical being you better prove it quick or I will......' Jess waved her rolling pin at the pair of them.

'Your name is Jess Bevan, you were born in this house, your mum's name is Joan, your friends are called Claire, Jamie, Amy and Sarah and you love Harry more than anything and you would give the world to have him back'.

Jess hesitated for a moment as she felt her guard drop. How did this stranger know so much?

'I don't believe you, you could have got that information from school records or something'.

'For trolls sake Jess, stop being so stubborn, you know I am real, look in to yourself, you know it'.

At this point Paul had had enough, Jess needed to understand what was happening. He pulled out a snow globe from his pocket and thrust it towards her.

'What is that?' She shouted, recoiling from it as if one touch of it would kill her.

'Just take it and look at it' Paul said firmly.

Jess was hesitant but she slowly reached out and took the snow globe off Paul. She looked into it but could not see a thing.

'What is so special about this all I can see is my reflection?'

'Shake it'.

Jess shook the snow globe hard and then looked at it again. As the snow fell down inside it, she could see images begin to appear, they were moving, it was, no it couldn't be, but it was, Jess couldn't believe what she was seeing with her own eyes, it was her and Harry's first kiss. There first kiss being played on a loop over and over in this thing. She couldn't believe she had forgot this and then she remembered it was at a gig, a music gig.

All of a sudden, her whole life time exposure to music flooded back into her head in one massive wave and with it, all the parts of her relationship with Harry that she had forgotten, it was all there again. She looked up at the two strangers in her living room, they were looking desperately at her for some recognition.

Santa spoke softly 'Now do you believe I am Santa?'

At that very moment Jess fainted and lay sprawled out on the floor. Paul turned to Santa.

'Well I think that went well'.

*

Santa and Paul stood over Jess as she sat slumped on the sofa still unconscious.

'How long are we meant to just wait here?'

'Well until she wakes up' Paul replied.

'And how long will that be?'

'How should I know? I haven't got a crystal ball'

'You are supposed to know everything, you are my head elf, you could have warned me she was going to faint'.

'Well I didn't know she was definitely going to faint but to be fair Santa the whole fabric of her reality has been ripped apart, its bound to make anyone feel a little bit light headed'

'Yeah I guess so'

As they watched on, Jess began to come round, she barely had her eyes open.

'Is that you mum? Ah you wouldn't believe it, I had the craziest dream'.

Santa interrupted her 'Nope, it was not a dream'.

Jess opened her eyes wide 'oh no' she mumbled.

Jess tried to get up but was too unsteady on her feet, without much resistance Paul sat her backdown. He looked at her and spoke calmly but firmly.

'Do you remember who we are now?'

'I think so'.

'And who is that?'

'Well he is Santa Clause and you are an elf. I remember hearing about you Santa, all the stories, everyone debating whether you were real and I remember all about Christmas now. But how, how could everyone forget about Christmas? How did I forget about it?'

Jess looked at the pair of them utterly confused. This last year had been one long drawn out moment of confusion but she felt like she couldn't comprehend anything now, she felt like she was losing her mind. Santa tried to settle her and then he began to explain everything.

'Exactly a year ago I was attacked by Crnobog, he is the god of darkness and ruler of the dead. When he attacked me, he also attacked Harry, he hurt Harry bad, he destroyed his love for you and his love for music, which as you now remember were the two biggest things to him in the world. As well as doing that he hurt me pretty bad too and he took away my reindeers and the sleigh. Because of that I couldn't deliver Christmas and that broke the world. That one night missed made everyone forget Christmas, love and music'

'But what can I do to change that and how did you know to come to me?'

'We read the letter you sent'.

'I haven't sent any letters'.

'Yes, you did, the one you sent in the fire'.

Jess's eyes widened as the penny finally dropped 'What, how? I saw that the letter burned up in front of my eyes'.

'Don't you remember doing it as a young child? You used to write letters to me and your mum and dad used to sit with you in front of the fire as you put them in and they told you that the smoke would send the letter to me'.

The forgotten memory came back to her, she was so glad to have it back, she had cherished those moments. Santa continued.

'Well they were not far wrong. The fire place at the North pole would pick your letters up and throw them out to me. Slightly singed sometimes but I always got them. Every single one. So, when this came, I knew it was a sign'.

'A sign of what?' Jess asked.

'A sign that you are the person that we need. We need you Jess. To save Christmas. To save the world.'

Jess paused for a moment unsure what she had just heard 'Uh, come again'.

Paul stepped in 'We need you to help us save the world'.

Jess burst out in nervous laughter, Paul and Santa exchanged looks, they didn't know how to deal with this. Jess clocked both of them looking confused.

'You two are confused? How do you think I feel? I have just found out that everything I believed in that I forgot about, is actually true and the rest of the world can't remember it and you want me to make the rest of the world remember. How? I have no magic powers, I am just a teenage girl who is too scared to even go out much these days.'

Santa knew he would have to be blunt with her.

'Hey nobody is just anything and you Jess, you are special! You have always been a beautiful soul but when the whole world went dark, you were the only light that shined on. You couldn't be broken even with the world against you, you remembered that love was the most important thing'.

'So, what do you want from me?'

'We need you to make Harry believe again, to know what you know and to fall in love with you'

'But he doesn't love me anymore' Jess stressed.

'He does, he just doesn't know it right now. Look we will be with you, just tell him everything, about the pair of you, all your memories and remember to tell him about Christmas and music. If you do that, he should remember and if he remembers, as the source of all of this, then that should save the world, so that everyone remembers'.

'Are you sure this will work?' Jess asked tentatively.

'We have to try'.

*

As Santa, Paul and Jess all neared Harry's house Jess began to feel a great sense of unease.

'I really don't think I can do this, I can not do this again, what if he says no? I can't put myself through that again'.

Santa just stood there, he didn't know what to say but Paul gently took her by the hand.

'We are right here by your side. I can't promise you this will be easy but we are not going anywhere'. He looked up to her and smiled softly. Jess took it on board, she wasn't alone. She squeezed Paul's hand and let it go.

She walked up to the door and the other two stood a short distance behind her. She readied herself, took a big deep breath and knocked on the door. A few moments passed, each moment feeling like a lifetime and then the door swung open and their stood Harry, he looked as beautiful as ever to Jess, to her he glowed. He looked at Jess and she looked at him but, in that moment, she did not know what to say and began to stutter, before she could properly say anything though and get any words out Harry interrupted.

'Jess I already told you it is over. Go away'.

He shut the door behind him. Jess just stood there in shock. She knew this would be hard but she didn't think that he would be this cold. After all that they were, it seemed there was nothing for her inside of him. Harry stood still leaning behind the other side of the door. What was she doing here? Despite living so close he hadn't seen her for nearly a year, why would she just come to his front door like that? And who were those two weirdos with her?

Santa prodded Jess who still had not moved.

'You need to tell him, tell him everything, even if it is through the door'.

Still not moving she whispered 'Ok' trying to hold back the tears.

'Harry, I know that the boy who loves me is still in there, the world might be an awful place right now but deep down you know it is not right. Please just come out here and let me show you. These two with me, they showed me that I was right about love and also that Santa Clause and Christmas is real and Harry there is this thing called music too. It is beautiful Harry, it's how we found each other remember? Heavy metal and rock music. The sounds that spoke to us individually and brought us together. Harry just think about, I know if you think hard about it enough you will remember'.

Jess threw every ounce of passion at that wooden door, she felt like her emotions had just been pulled out from inside her. She had nothing left to give but the door remained shut and that was it. Jess gave up, she turned around and looked at Santa and Paul, her eyes were red and puffy and she gave a half-hearted shrug.

'I did the best I could'.

Paul and Santa stood their speechless, she had done all she could but just as they were about to throw in the towel the door opened and out came Harry.

'What's this thing you said about Santa Clause?'

Jess couldn't believe it, he had come out, she run up to him and flung her arms around him, he didn't return the favour and just stood there, still waiting for her to stop, finally she let go.

'I knew it, I knew you still loved me'.

'No, I do not Jess' Harry said coldly, cutting Jess in two.

'But….'

'What did you say about Santa though? When I've been hearing his name on tv, it's been making me go all weird, like I've been having hallucinations and that'.

'Santa is real. He is right here' Jess turned around and pointed to Santa.

Santa smiled 'Hey Harry, it's been a while'.

Harry turned back to Jess 'Him?'

'Yes'

'And who is the other one?'

'That's Paul, his head elf'.

'What's that?'

'Like his second in command. They are both here to help us save Christmas and put the world back to how it was'.

'Them two?'

'Yes'.

'They are the worst pairing I have ever seen, they look like a polar opposite double act from a bad 80's sitcom. No offence guys'.

Both Santa and Paul looked at each other.

'I have taken some offence to that' Santa said.

'Yeah me too' Paul added.

Jess grabbed both his hands and looked him in the eyes.

'They are as real as it gets. But it is only us who can actually change the world Harry. You have to trust me. You need to love me just like I know you once did'.

'I can't even if I wanted too, I can't feel what you want me to feel. I'm sorry' He let her hands go.

Paul decided to intervene, he got the globe back out and put it in Harry's hand.

'Shake it'.

Harry obliged. As he watched the snow fall, he began to see images play out inside the snow globe. It was him and Jess, they were together and then they were kissing. He watched it over and over on a loop. It fascinated him, he could not remember that moment though. Was it even real? Or was it just some weird video that they had put into this thing?

'Do you see it now?' Jess asked, as if begging for the answer she so desperately wanted.

'No, I don't. I can't remember that, is it real?'

Jess wanted to scream at him and slap him across his stupid face, how couldn't he see it?

'Harry you must see it! How can't you? Seeing that brought everything back to me, I've showed you everything I can think of there is nothing left to show you or say to you'.

'I'm sorry, I know you are trying everything but I don't know what you want me to feel, no matter what you say or what you do, I can not feel this love you want me to feel. I want to know what love is, I want you to show me'.

'That's it'. Jess shouted.

'What?'

'Shut up' She demanded, in that moment, Jess grabbed Harry's face and kissed him like her life depended on it. For a second Harry wanted to pull away, what was she doing? But then it all started flooding back to him, all the love he felt for Jess, he remembered music again and Christmas, every moment surged through his brain as he kissed Jess back passionately. He couldn't believe he had let her go and he never wanted this kiss to end. When they finally pulled away from each other Jess spoke first.

'Well?'

Harry took a long breath out 'I think I remember'.

But at that moment Harry's eyes glazed over and he fainted to the snowy floor. Jess looked back panic stricken. Santa just shrugged his shoulders.

'Must have been one hell of a kiss'.

Chapter 11

Harry was sat upright on the front door step where he had laid unconscious one year ago. He had now seemed to have come around a bit from his faint.

'You ok Harry?' Jess asked.

'Yeah I just feel a little light headed'.

Paul opened up his rucksack and got out a flask. He took off the lid and poured its contents out.

'Here have some of this coco it will help with the shock.' He passed Harry the drink.

'Thanks' Harry said, nodding as he took the coco.

'And I would stay seated for a little bit longer too, your whole reality has just been exposed as a lie, so you might feel a bit unbalanced'.

'I will bare that in mind' Harry quipped taking another sip of coco.

He looked around him, he had Jess, an elf and the actual Santa Clause surrounding him.

'Well you were right all along Jess, Santa is real? You know she never stopped believing in you Santa.'

'Yeah I know, she is special'.

Jess blushed, she hesitated for a second but then she knew she had to ask.

'Santa, how are we going to know if it has worked, there is only us here?'

Paul and Santa had looked at each other. They didn't know what to say and Paul cursed himself, this was the problem when proper plans were not made. Then he remembered, he had packed the Christmas spirit level, that would tell them.

Paul searched through his rucksack once more but as he got nearer to finding the spirit level everything changed and they could all feel it. There was a rustling in the trees, the earth began to shake underneath their foot and the wind grew louder and louder, growling all around them, but amongst all of this Santa could hear a sound oh so familiar too, then he appeared, being carried by the reindeers in the sleigh. It was Crnobog.

The sleigh came to a stop right in front of them and Crnobog disembarked from it. Slowly, taking his time as the rest watched on. He was in complete control. Crnobog began rummaging in the back of the sleigh and as he did so he began to sing in a jolly tone 'Jingle bells, jingle bells, jingle all the way, oh what fun it is to ride in a one-horse open sleigh, hey'. This he did completely with his back to them all as if they weren't even there. Harry and Jess were frozen solid with fear. Santa and Paul just didn't know how to react, what was Crnobog planning?

He then turned around with a crown in his hand, waving it around like it was worth nothing, when it was indeed priceless. He then placed it on his head, but the crown didn't fit and was lob sided as draped over Crnobog's head and shoulders was what looked like the fur of a wild bear.

'What do you think of the crown Santa? Suits me don't you think? And this delightful bear coat, nice isn't it? I was just letting it know its life was about to come to an end when I noticed what you were up to so it didn't get the ending it deserved. You really should think about others before yourself Santa, very needless for this creature to have such a death.'

Harry couldn't work out what was going on but he wanted answers.

'Hey who are you?' He shouted.

Crnobog barely flicked his wrist as he bellowed 'Silence boy!'

Harry flew through the air and landed twenty feet away by an old tree.

'Harry!' Jess screamed as she ran to him.

Santa remained still, his eyes locked on Crnobog. He hadn't said a word but his face was filled with a silent rage that Paul had never seen before.

'This sleigh is very nice isn't it. I can see why you were so found of it' Crnobog smirked but Santa remained as still as a statue.

'How have you been keeping Santa? We didn't really get to chat the last time we met. You are really not looking great, you seemed to have aged terribly by the look of you, I would have thought with no work load and all the elves gone you would finally be relaxed and care free but clearly not. Don't go worrying about your elves now, they are working for me and I keep them occupied so they don't get bored. I do find throwing them in the lava keeps them nicely on their toes, you should try that with the ones you still got'.

Crnobog paused briefly.

'Oh, that's right, sorry all your elves are dead now, aren't they?'.

Paul lunged forward, he wanted to destroy Crnobog and make him feel all the pain that he had felt in this last year but Santa held his arm across him to stop the onslaught to which Paul quickly did but not before Crnobog spotted it.

'Oh, come now, did that make you angry little fella? Do you feel all sad because all your little friends are dead?'

Paul dug his feet into the snow trying his hardest to hold himself back as Crnobog just chuckled to himself. Santa then finally spoke, he didn't shout or scream, but he just spoke softly and calmly to Crnobog.

'Yeah your right it seems I have aged a little but I tell you what would make me feel a whole lot better, it would be if you were to call all this off and let things go back to how they were'.

'And why would I do that? What benefit is that to me?'

'Because you know it is the right thing to do'.

'The right thing? Because you have always known what the right thing to do is haven't you. You have always considered yourself better than me, ever since the beginning when it was just us' Crnobog's voice grew louder and louder with each passing sentence.

Jess and Harry had walked back into ear shot defiantly unafraid of Crnobog Jess spoke 'Santa what does he mean by just you two? How do you know this thing?'

Santa responded quickly 'We have got a long history' but as he said this, he couldn't quite meet Jess's eye.

Crnobog laughed 'Now Santa why would you lie like that? Where is that sense of truth and justice that you always claim to have hmmm. Gone it seems. You see they call me the evil one but at least I have never been a hypocrite unlike you. Isn't that right brother?'

As Crnobog dropped this bombshell he grinned from ear to ear, as he watched the result of his words unfold in front of him. Harry and Jess were frozen in confusion, baffled by the revelation, Santa looked down at the ground, his secret now revealed and Paul who had been standing by his side began to back away.

'He was your brother all along and you said nothing'. Paul shouted, his voice cracking in emotion as he continued to distance himself away from Santa.

'Paul I….' Santa began to protest desperately but Paul interrupted.

'No Santa, no. You, you betrayed us, you lied to us, you never told us about this threat. We trusted you'.

Crnobog chirped in with another blow 'Yep. Betrayal, lies and deceit. That is old Saint Nicholas by here. That is his game. Between us we used to get up to all sorts of great mischief, causing trouble all around the world. But then you went to the council of gods about me and you got me banished to the world of the dead. All at the hand of my own brother'.

Santa retorted back 'I had to do it, you were out of control'.

'We were a team, we were going to take over the world together'.

'But what is the point of taking over the world if there is nothing good in it. You wanted to destroy everyone and everything'.

'That is the only way Santa. But don't stand their and make out that we are the opposites that you claim.'

'I would never do that'.

'Because you are just as evil as me'.

'I have my regrets, that I agree are many, but I am not as evil as you are'.

'Is that so. Then why all holy one did you offer your elves to me, just after you as you so called it acquired them?'

Paul felt sick 'Santa is this true?'

Santa pleaded with Paul to see the truth 'No it is not Paul I promise you, he is telling a lie'.

'I would not be so quick to believe him elf, how do you think I knew how to get you all so quick? How to get in the North Pole and even how you perish without soulmates? I knew it all because he told me everything. He wanted me to have you lot, he wanted to come to me and leave this Christmas life behind and takeover the world with me to make it dark. He doesn't see you as some helpers in a magical land making the world a better place. He sees you as slaves worthy of nothing more than a tool to facilitate his ego'.

Paul couldn't handle this any longer. He had been lied to all this time. All the elves had been lied too and as head elf he had walked all of them to their deaths by working with Santa. The rage inside Paul had become astronomical, he could feel his whole body intoxicated by it. The magic of all his ancestors and all his fellow elves began to course through his veins and was begging for a release. Santa looked at Paul and saw him in a way he had never before and this this scared him in a way he had never felt before, this was Paul, Paul who hadn't felt an ounce of anger in a thousand years.

He pleaded with him 'Paul, please don't listen to him it is all lies! He is just trying to divide us. Trying to manipulate us and play us off each other, it's all a fame to him'.

Crnobog decided to turn the knife in again 'Do you know why you have never found love Paul?'

Paul looked at Crnobog. Confused more than ever. 'What?'

Crnobog lowered his voice and zoned in on Paul as if locking in to his prey 'You never found love, not because the universe decided you wasn't destined for a soulmate. It was because Santa here killed your soulmate before you even knew who they were. You are not just an unlovable freak Paul, you are an unlovable freak with a dead soulmate'.

Paul was visibly shaking and blue light started glowing from his fingertips. Santa looked at Paul, his eyes pleading with him not to believe.

'Paul Please don't believe him I would never have done that to you. I love you and there is nothing wrong with you. You are loved by me and everyone who knows you'.

Crnobog spat back in retort 'Don't listen to his manipulation, he wants you to feel indebted to him, he did it so you had nothing, so that you would become his head elf with no distractions, he has manipulated you all your life, he's treated you like a slave and you will never be free with him'.

Stuck in the middle of the two of them, his violent shaking stopped and the lights from his finger tips stopped glowing. He twisted his head in the direction of Santa. His eyes were red just like the reindeers, Santa's heart dropped, Crnobog's words alone had corrupted him.

Then Paul shouted out 'Santa! Be ready!'

Paul twisted himself towards Crnobog and struck out a stream of blue light, hitting Crnobog and sending him flying backwards. Paul felt on fire, he had never used this battle magic inside of him. He looked towards Santa whose eyes were wide with shock at what Paul had just done.

'You believe me?' Santa exclaimed.

Paul nodded at Santa 'Always'.

Crnobog got back up to his feet quickly and then began to raise himself in the air, as he did so the wind all around them began to growl and everything started to go black, to the point that none of them could barely see. Then Crnobog's voice echoed out.

'You love this world and these pathetic creatures more than me Santa. You will regret ever abandoning me!'

Santa felt himself get thrown in the air and then he smashed into something hard but he had no idea what this was. He still couldn't see. He could hear the wind growls and he could hear the screams from the others pierce through the darkness, each one hurting him more. He got up but unable to see he had no direction. The wind echoed the screams all around. Santa was powerless, he hit out a bolt of battle magic, trying to light up his surroundings but it was as useful as lighting a wet match. But then he saw a glint of blue light ahead. It came, then went, then it came again. It was Paul, he was doing the same thing as Santa.

Santa aimed the best he could and threw out his light towards the light he could see ahead, desperately hoping he didn't hit Paul in the process. The first one missed, not connecting to anything but when Santa threw out his light again so did Paul and this collision brought the daylight back to this battlefield again. Crnobog was now on display again and he hit out his dark energy at the pair of them. As he did so Santa and Paul through their energy towards him and it connected with his energy, creating a dome of dark around them all that still remained light inside just like the last time.

As Santa and Paul locked in to the battle with Crnobog they could feel his power was so strong, even stronger than last time. The energy he had fed off through the world becoming this dark, cold and devoid of love place had made him so powerful and they were struggling to battle on as they began to feel his power submerge them, the darkness was creeping closer and closer. But just as the dark energy began to dance across their chest's they felt Jess and Harry by there by their sides. Harry next to Santa tried to shout out encouragement.

'You can beat him Santa I believe in you, you fought against him once, you can do this, you can win'.

Santa kept pushing on, barely holding off Crnobog, the encouragement was clearly not working. Jess looked on to this lost, feeling powerless to help, but she knew she needed to do something. Santa and Paul had just shown her the truth and she was not about to go back to a lie. But as she looked at Paul the dark energy had taken over his light and a sea of blackness was pouring across his chest, filling up as more dark energy poured into Paul. Jess could see the light going from his eyes and as they fixed on to Jess, she knew what she had to do.

Jess threw herself in front of Paul and screamed out in pain as the darkness hit her. She could feel it trying to tear her soul apart but she would not let this battle be lost. Jess threw her hands forward for reasons she didn't know why and a stream of red-light energy soared out of her and it didn't stop.

Crnobog was taken aback, he shuffled back and had to dig his heels in to the ground to stand strong. Santa and Jess had now managed to get their white and red lights over halfway against Crnobog's dark light. Santa glanced out of the corner of his eye towards Jess, he couldn't believe what he was seeing, he had never seen a person be able to summon this energy. Jess was struggling to believe it too. What in the name of elves was this coming out of her? But while she was unsure of that she had never felt more certain about what she had to do, so she continued to battle on.

Between Jess and Santa, they pushed on and with their energy halfway over it continued to get closer and closer to Crnobog. Battling on both fronts he was struggling to fight them. The sheer force of the energy in this battle began to break the ground below them, making Jess wobble and this one moment made her lose grip on

Crnobog and with this he threw his arm out sending Jess hurtling through the sky.

Now it was just Santa Clause and Crnobog left but with Crnobog back to one on one he was in control again. The ground that had began to rumble was now breaking up and a massive hole was now in the middle of them and just like before it growled and hissed. The portal to hell opened again and was the only thing that separated the duelling pair as it hissed and spat from its depths.

The hole grew larger and larger, edging ever so closer to Santa who was now on the edge of it, but then just as it looked like Santa was about to be hit by Crnobog's energy another portal began to appear but this time it was too the side of them and it was in the air and didn't glow red but of every colour in the universe.

As the portal grew bigger Santa realised what it was and then flying through the portal came Mrs Clause and Tracey. As Mrs Clause came flying through, she threw herself at Santa pushing him out of the way of Crnobog's energy and breaking the duel, with Tracey behind catching Crnobog off guard, she launched a stream of battle energy at him which sent him flying backwards.

 As Santa got to his feet, he could see Tracey and Mrs Clause in front of hm and he had never been happier to see them, they had just saved his life.

He gasped 'Thank you, you just saved me but how did you just do that, how did you get through the portal?'

Both Mrs Clause and Tracey glanced at each other and spoke simultaneously 'We have our ways'.

But before there reunion had even begun Crnobog had risen to his feet and he flew himself over the bubbling hole below and headed straight for Mrs Clause. He grabbed her by the throat and carried her high in to the air leaving Santa and Tracey helpless below.

'I knew you would make an appearance. You could never leave him be with me. You are nothing more than a meddler who got lucky but your luck is over now. I am going to make you watch as I take the last ounces of life out of Santa, maybe then you will know what it is like to see the one you love die in front of your very eyes'.

With that Crnobog slammed Mrs Clause into the ground and lunged towards Santa, throwing Tracey out of the way in the process. Unopposed now and one to one with Santa, he no longer resorted to using energy but instead he put his hands around Santa Clause's throat and squeezed as hard as he could as he lay on top of him on the floor.

He stared in to his eyes, the eyes of a brother he once loved and continued to pile on the pressure to his neck. Santa couldn't breath any more, his lungs were on fire, fighting to try and regain an ounce of air. He began punching out hitting Crnobog as hard as he could but the blows did nothing to stop him, each one was weaker and weaker but then out of the corner of his eye he could see Mrs Clause at full steam flying towards Santa and Crnobog who spotted her as well. He unleashed his grip and threw out his dark energy towards her but he missed and she threw herself into Crnobog, but as Santa's lungs breathed a sigh of relief as air greeted them, he could only watch as the tackling Mrs Clause holding onto Crnobog flew over him and they both plunged into the depths of hells.

Santa screamed out like an animal 'NOOOOOOO'.

He tried to scramble to his feet, he had to go after her, he had to go in to the depths of hell to save Mrs Clause but before he could get to his feet the hole disappeared, the wind and growling stopped and the darkness lifted.

Santa was on his knees staring at the earth which had just swallowed up his world.

He screamed out 'No this is not real!'

He began clawing at the snow and earth in desperation, all he could think was that he would dig his way to hell if he had too, as he clawed with his hands pointlessly.

Tracey then screamed out at him 'Santa come here quick'.

He ran over to Tracey who was cradling Paul on the floor as Jess and Harry were knelt down next to him. Paul looked a mess, he had suffered a direct hit of Crnobog's dark powers and it had resulted in a huge gash from the bottom of his stomach all the way up his body and across his face and the wound was deep. Santa knelt down next to Paul and held his hand as he began to cry uncontrollably, he couldn't lose them both.

'Paul tell me what to do?'

Paul barely able to keep his eyes open looked up at Santa and raised a smile.

'I don't think this is one either of us can fix this time big man'. He spoke softly through each struggling breath.

'No, I won't have this, you must know a way, please Paul I can't lose you, I need you more than anything'.

'You have never needed me Santa, you survived before me and you will after'.

'I can't Paul, I can't. If I lose you and I've just lost her, I can't do this, I can't carry on'.

Paul grimaced in pain but he squeezed Santa's hand as hard as he could.

'You must carry on Santa. Do the one thing I always ask of you that you never do. Keep to the schedule and get the job done'.

Paul withered in pain again and he could barely get any air to his lungs but he continued to smile at Santa as a single tear began to come down his face.

'Santa, in a world full of darkness it has been my greatest honour to be a candle. It is your time now to show the world how to shine again'.

As he finished his words, the lights in his eyes went out and he became limp. Santa closed his eyes with his fingers and gently let go of his hand. Several minutes passed and nobody said a word, they all just continued to kneel together, lost in complete shock at the events they had just witnessed. They had come so close to saving the world but now they had no idea where to go from here. They had no idea what would work to save the whole world.

The only thing Santa did know was that he was not going to leave Paul here. As he got up, he scooped the elf's limp body and began to carry it back towards the reindeers and sleigh. He walked past the reindeers and his heart was heavy as he saw the red still in their eyes which accompanied their now black exterior. Santa then carefully placed Paul in the back of the sleigh and he removed his jacket draping it over Paul's body.

As he looked at him, he whispered. 'Look at you hey, you would have made the best father Christmas, I hope you know I did love you, you were my brother'.

Santa then walked back to the front of the reindeer pack. He looked at Rudolph but could see no recognition in the reindeer's eyes. He had only one idea of how to change that. He held Rudolph with both his hands on each side of his head and then kissed the top of it, he held this for a moment and then let go. As he did so the eyes of Rudolph began to change, back to their normal colour and the black fur that had engulfed Rudolph faded away. The Rudolph Santa knew was back, a little worse for wear but back all the same. Rudolph's eyes widened as the reindeer snorted and bobbed at Santa.

'I knew you were still in there'.

Santa then began to go to each of the reindeer and repeated the process until all of them were back to normal. It was small but it gave him some comfort to see his reindeers were no longer suffering now, but as he looked at them, he knew he still didn't know what to do. How could he return love to this world, especially as he had just seen all that he loved in it be wiped out?

As Santa continued to ponder Jess spotted an object in the snow. It was the snow globe she had been given by Paul. She picked it up and shook it once more. She watched as her and Harry's first kiss played out over and over in front of her. She got lost in it, remembering just how wonderful that moment felt.

As the snow began to settle, the images stopped. Jess lifted the snow globe up to restart it again and she spotted something underneath the globe. There was writing on it. She read it and her heart skipped a beat.

'Santa, I know how we can make everyone believe again'.

'How?'

'It's on the snow globe. Paul must have written this down back at the North Pole. Come look'.

Santa, Tracey and Harry all gathered around Jess and looked at this snow globe. She turned it over to show Paul's writing underneath to which Santa read aloud.

'If Harry alone doesn't revive the Christmas spirit, the only way must be through the world being reminded all at once. Only with the sheer force of everyone remembering, even for a second, do we stand a chance. The world is apart and it must be brought together.'

'It must be brought together?' Tracey repeated, unsure of how to solve this.

'Jess this is all well and good but we don't know how to do that and we don't know how much time we have before Crnobog comes back for us and when he does, I'm not sure we can survive him again'.

Tracey then realised what they had to do.

'I have an idea'.

Chapter 12

'London?' They all questioned.

'London' Tracey repeated.

'Why London though, what is there that is going to help us change the world?' Harry asked.

'The London Eye'.

'But what is so special about that it's just a giant Ferris wheel'. Jess declared.

'No, it is not, you know that bit in the middle that holds up the wheel. Well that has got a transmitter in it. That transmitter is powerful enough that it can transmit to every device in the entire world'.

Santa was dumbstruck 'How do you know about this? Also how do I not know about it?'

'The MOEI learned about it during its creation, it wasn't something we though you would ever need to know about to be honest Santa, you keep your identity a secret so you wouldn't need to broadcast yourself to the world'.

'What's the MOEI?' Harry queried.

'The Ministry of Elf Investigation. It is a specialised investigatory unit. They specialise in gaining intel on threats to the North Pole and general world peace'.

'So like elf spies?' Harry asked.

Tracey looked at Harry 'Yeah something like that'.

Harry saying that made Tracey think about the unit for a moment. She remembered a mission she had done with them, where they had to infiltrate an explorer group as they were about to stumble on to the North Pole. She inner giggled to herself. A bonk of a candy cane to the head was always a great idea on a mission, it knocked them out and they couldn't remember a thing. Also watching Jenny from wrapping division tie up a big burly explorer and put a bow on his head would always remain a lasting memory. She always found time for a bow.

'So, what exactly is your plan then?' Santa asked.

'We need to get to London, once at the London Eye we can transmit a message to the whole world. That way it might just work, everyone getting the same message at once'.

'But what would we all say exactly?'

'Not us Santa, you, I think we need to have you give it and yes, I know, I know you shouldn't be seen but we can work out how to fix that later but you are Christmas, it really could only be you who truly fixes this world'.

'But what would I say to fix the world its not as simple as saying I'm Santa. Choose Christmas. Choose Love'.

Tracey paused for a second, yes she knew what he needed to say 'You need to tell people what it means to love, what Christmas really means to you, about how music makes your soul feel. Just tell them all about that and speak from the heart, I know it will be hard but I will be right by your side'.

'Do you think it will work?'

'If the world sees the man who has loved them unconditionally all these years pour his heart out to them, it might just work'.

Santa smiled at Tracey, even in this his darkest moment she knew just what to say. This was about way more than just him, this was about everyone who was in pain right now.

'Well we better get going then'.

They all got in to the sleigh and sat down. Santa felt the reigns in his hands, his heart raced as he felt the adrenaline rush through him, he was where he belonged again. Harry and Jess looked at each other. Jess knew this was about saving the world but she couldn't contain her excitement.

'Harry we are in the sleigh, Santa's sleigh!' She screamed quietly to him.

Harry couldn't quite believe it either. He had Jess back and was sitting in Santa's sleigh all within the last twenty minutes. It was a lot to take in. Santa at the front took a big deep breath and for the first time in a year he whipped the reigns of this sleigh. The sleigh launched forward and flew in to the air, going higher and higher, the wind blew into Santa's face as they headed to London but just as the reindeers got to full speed Santa remembered and threw the sleigh back around.

'Santa what are you doing?' Tracey shouted.

'We forgot John!'

Within moments they were back at Jess's house. John was still standing there blissfully unaware of everything that had just happened.

'John come here' Santa called out to him.

John hobbled over to the sleigh, he pushed in next to Rudolph and began to strap his reigns on himself.

'No John get in the back'

John threw off his reigns and walked to the back of the sleigh, as he clambered his old self in to the sleigh it sank down in protest at the old reindeer's weight. Just as he got in, he slipped and fell forward, his antlers smashing in to the back of Jess and Harry's head.

'Ouch' They both shouted out.

John decided to apologise to them by slobbering over both of them, giving them massive wet licks to the face. Santa looked back towards the pair of them and John. The reindeer seemed very content with his place at the back of the sleigh. Santa looked forward again and got ready for a second time, he snapped the reigns and off they flew, all the way to London, to save the world.

'Hold on we are coming in hot!' Santa shouted out.

They all gripped on to the sleigh for their lives as the reindeers hurtled down to the ground. As the sleigh hit the floor the sheer force of the landing sent it back in to the air again and with it all their occupants were ejected and flew through the air, Santa and Tracey, then followed by Harry and Jess behind with John coming up from the rear who hadn't remembered he could fly. Bang, thud, bang, bang, thud!

They all crashed to the floor with Tracey having a soft landing as she fell in to a dazed Santa. Harry came off a little worse though as just after he fell hard to the floor, the big burly ball of fur landed directly on top of him and unfortunately that was not Jess. As Harry lay their feeling crushed by the furry jack hammer, John had quickly got up and began to lick his face again hoping this would quickly dull the pain. It did not, he now was just wet and ached.

Jess stood over him and pulled him up 'come on now you can't stay there all day, we got a job to do'.

With them all on their feet they looked up to the reason they were here. The London Eye. It stood their towering above them on the edge of the River Thames, from the bottom this definitely looked bigger than a normal Ferris wheel Jess thought.

'So how exactly are we supposed to get up there?' Santa asked.

Tracey had to think. It was the middle of the night and it was all blocked off and it was not like they could just climb up to the middle of the London Eye anyway. Then the light bulb moment struck.

'The bag!'

Santa stared at her confused 'What do you mean the bag?'

'The bag, the one that Paul brought where is it? That's got what I need in it'.

Jess went to the sleigh and got the bag that Paul had got the snow globe out of and passed it to Tracey. She could not understand what would be in there that could solve this problem though, it felt completely empty even though it looked full.

Tracey put the bag on the floor and stuck her head inside, her voice began to echo from inside it 'Paul really does prepare for everything doesn't he'.

'An elf needs to be prepared for every situation' Santa repeated Paul's words as he glanced at the sleigh, remembering Paul was still in the back of it.

'Does not make it easy for me to find a single thing'. Tracey moaned as she went further into the bag with now only her legs still visible.

As the rest of the group waited Tracey huffed and puffed and began throwing items out of the bag. Every item possible started flying through the air; plasters, ropes, biscuits, flares, bottles of water, candy canes, mistletoe, books, broccoli and a rubber chicken were all strewn out across before Tracey abruptly stopped.

'Ah yes, just what I needed!' Tracey stood up with her tools in hand. A screwdriver, a drill and Sellotape.

'Um how is Sellotape going to help?' Jess enquired nervously, it looked like Tracey had lost her mind.

Tracey looked at her and winked 'Like this'. Then with the Sellotape in one hand, she launched it in a curling motion. As the Sellotape began to fly off its base towards the middle of the London Eye Tracey went after it, flying through the air she circled around it and then landed right in the centre. The rest of them looked up from the ground shocked at how she had just got up there.

'Fifty years in wrapping back in the day, you never lose it!' She shouted down.

She then began working on getting to the transmitter, drilling away just at a weak point that the MOEI had found out about when they discovered the world transmitter plans. After some precise drilling and fiddling with the screwdriver the middle of the London eye opened and inside Tracey could see it sitting there, the transmitter. She breathed a sigh of relief, she was so glad it was here, although this transmitter didn't look anything like an ordinary one, this looked like a candle but this one would not smell nice and light up a room, it would bring the world back to how it should be.

Tracey grabbed the candle transmitter and with one sweeping motion she flew off the London Eye and landed safely back at its base in front of the group.

'There you go' Tracey said holding up the transmitter for the rest of the group to see.

Santa, Harry, Jess and even John all exchanged looks, then Harry whispered to Jess.

'Isn't that a candle?'

Jess looked back at him, unable to elevate his concerns. Santa however took a more direct approach, he grabbed hold of it and inspected it, his frustration was clear.

'You made me drag us all here for this, this isn't a transmitter it is a ruddy candle!'

'No, it is not you big dope look'. She took it off him and pulled at the end. It popped off and inside the candle object was wires upon wires and a glowing blue light shining through.

'See' She exclaimed holding the end up to them all.

'How are you going to get it to transmit to everyone in the world though. We don't have any camera or radio equipment or anything?' Jess asked.

'Have you got your phone on you?'

'Yeah'.

'Pass it here'.

Jess passed her phone to Tracey who started playing with the wires and the phone at ultra-speed. Her hands were all but a blur as she moved between the transmitter and the phone. She rearranged the wires and tapped away on the phone, strange sequences of numbers flashed across the screen, Jess's eyes widened, it was like she was trying to hack in to something.

'Hey you trying to hack in to the CIA or something?' Harry Joked.

Tracey laughed 'Please the CIA's security is a joke'.

She continued to type and fiddle with the wires and then she was finished. She passed the phone and transmitter to Jess who took them tentatively as if she was holding a bomb.

'That should work now. I have adjusted the transmitter system so it is connected to your phone. Once you press record that will transmit to every device in the world. TV's, phones, radios, ice cream van speakers, you name it, it will transmit to it. All you have to do is hold it up and video Santa'.

Jess nodded. Tracey looked towards Santa.

'Are you ready Santa?'

'Ready as I will ever be' He replied in as a cool of a voice as he could although on the inside, he couldn't be more nervous.

Tracey then turned back to Jess and nodded, who nodded back and pressed record. Santa tried to gather his thoughts and remembered what Tracey had told her. Speak from the heart.

'Um hey world, uh I am not sure if you know who I am, but uh I am Santa. Yeah, I actually do exist. I am real. I have actually been around for a very long time now bringing joy to you all, but last year, well to be honest I let you down. I lost and that meant you lost. You lost Christmas, love and music. Right now, you have not got a clue what that is but let me tell you, they are so very special'.

Santa began to choke up a little but he managed to regain his composure. He looked at Tracey, his only elf left, then at Harry and Jess, the first two people who had found love again and had their whole life ahead of them.

'Love, you see is the most beautiful, purest thing. It can hurt more than you could ever imagine but it will make you feel more joy and happiness than you every thought you deserved. And that deep down is what Christmas is all about. I do it because I love you all unconditionally, all I have ever tried to do is spread a little bit of that joy to make other feels they are not forgotten, children and adult alike and you have always done that for each other too. You all don't even realise that tonight is the night that I deliver presents to you usually, but instead I am hear, delivering this message. So please, look within you, just for a moment and try to feel what you know you have lost, remember it and hold on to it as hard as you can no matter how much it hurts, because you need love. You may not think it but you do, this is not about me and Christmas because without love Christmas doesn't even exist. No, this is about you, so please look in to yourself and please remember'.

Santa breathed out heavily, he felt emotionally spent after that but all he could do now was pray it would work. Jess pressed stop on the record button and lowered the phone, for a few moments they just stood there in complete silence, until eventually Harry broke the silence.

'When will we know If it has worked?'

Tracey glanced at Santa 'Do you know if Paul packed the Christmas spirit reader?'

'I think so'.

Tracey went back to the bag and once again began rummaging through with half her body inside. She grunted and groaned as bangs and pops could be heard coming from inside it before she then lifted herself up, holding what looked like a thermometer in her hand, but it was actually the Christmas spirit level reader. However, any joy that had been gained in finding it, quickly disappeared as they all could clearly see the reading. It was not rising. It was a big fat zero.

'It didn't work' Tracey declared

None of them said a thing, they all dropped their heads in disappointment. There was not anything else they could do Santa thought, he had tried his best, he spoke from his heart to the world, trying to explain to them love as best as he could but he had failed. Yes, Harry and Jess had discovered each other again but they were at the centre of the whole thing so maybe they were just lucky. Regardless of them it was clear Christmas had been lost forever'.

'Wait!' Tracey shouted out.

They all looked at her confused.

'Santa, how could we be so stupid?' Words are not going to bring Christmas back. Remember what I said back at the North Pole, it is music, that is what is going to work. Music is beyond words, it is indescribable and that is what love and Christmas is!'

Santa agreed with her but there was a flaw in her thinking 'I get that but the world lost music, it was erased. It is not like I can just press play on some classic rock songs and boom the world is fixed'.

'You are going to have do it'.

'What?'

'You are going to have to do it Santa. You need to sing and play guitar to the world. There is one in that bag I saw it earlier and Jess you need to start recording again. We are not giving up, this is not over until the fat man sings.'

Tracey went over to the bag and after some quick rummaging she pulled out the guitar. She whispered to herself 'Thank you for remembering Paul'.

She passed the guitar to Santa who held it in his hands and admired it for a moment. This was the guitar that might just save the world. Jess fiddled with her phone and then got it steady and pointed it towards Santa.

'What do I play?' He looked around hoping for an answer, it was not an easy question with what was at stake but Tracey replied swiftly.

'Play the one'.

'The one?'

'Do you really think there is a more appropriate tune for right now?'

'I guess not'.

He looked at Jess and nodded. She hit record.

'Hey world it's me again. I know you still don't believe in me but please just listen to this'.

But just then as Santa struck the first note on the guitar, a great big growl could be heard. He knew straight away, what it was, it was Crnobog again. As Santa and the others frantically looked around to see him from the River Thames a whirlpool began to form, growing rapidly it grew larger and larger until it was as wide as the river itself. Just like before with the hole in the ground, a red glow could be seen from its depths as it hissed and spit, the wind was also battering them, it was so powerful the group struggled to stay on the ground, but unlike previous times it didn't get darker. Then suddenly from the whirlpool itself Crnobog and Mrs Clause flew out of it and high in to the sky.

Santa could not believe it. Mrs Clause was alive and right at this moment she was flying through the air fighting Crnobog, but that was not the only shocking thing as just behind them all the elves from hell poured out of the whirlpool. Hundreds upon hundreds of them all coming out and then landing right in front of the group, who all stood their stunned. The elves had returned. And right in front was the most important elf to Tracey, her beloved Darren.

'Hey lovely' he smiled at her.

She cried and ran to him but there was no time to enjoy the embrace as Crnobog and Mrs Clause came hurtling down towards them all. As they smashed in to the ground together, they both quickly rose to their feet. Santa had no idea where Mrs Clause's god like strength had come from but now, they stood shoulder to shoulder with the might of all behind them against just one. Crnobog.

He launched his darkness towards her as she replied in kind with her light as they engaged in battle once more. They were both equally matched as the battle raged on. As they continued, she shouted to Santa.

'The music Santa, you have to do the music!'

At that moment Paul's bag began to shake violently and guitars began to fly out from it. Hundreds of them flying through the air and all landing in the hands of Jess, Harry, Tracey and every single elf who now all stood their behind Mrs Clause and Santa.

Santa with still his guitar in hand shouted towards Jess 'Jess it's time to hit the record again'.

With her free hand she grabbed her phone and pressed record. Then in unison they all began to play.

'NOOOO' Crnobog bellowed from his depths as the music knocked him backwards, allowing Mrs Clause's light to gain on him.

They continued to play, chord after chord they struck the guitars, making the most beautiful sounds and with each chord Crnobog became weaker and weaker. Around the world people began to listen as their devices were interrupted and slowly, they started to realise what it was they could hear. It was music. From Toronto to Auckland the world was beginning to remember. They were remembering everything; their first Christmas, their favourite song, their first dance with their wives and husbands, it was flooding back to every soul, they remembered music, they remembered love and they remembered Santa Clause.

Back at the site of the London Eye Crnobog was struggling, the light was too powerful. He dug his heels in and pushed back against Mrs Clause and her band with all his might and he began to gain ground, but just at that moment a portal began to emerge at the side of them just like the one that Mrs Clause and Tracey had come through to save Santa.

Mrs Clause could not believe her eyes, who could be coming through this portal. It had appeared to her and Tracey out of nowhere when she begged the universe to let her help save Santa, she had known then in her soul he was in danger, but everyone was here, Santa and all the elves, everyone she cared about who loved her enough to summon that power that she could think of was here. Then through the portal they began to come, all the elves that had perished, that had been broken at the loss of their soulmates, they all came pouring through the portal, followed by the unicorns, the trolls and even the goblins. The whole of the North Pole was here and was not going down without a fight. As they all poured in Paul's bag shook violently, as further guitars flew out to all that could play them, adding further pressure to Crnobog but he just would not go down.

Then Santa heard a voice by his side that he thought he would never hear again.

'You still can't play a good rift Santa'.

He looked to his side. It was Paul. He did not know what to say, he had his friend back. Words could never describe that.

'How?' Is all he could master.

'I don't know what forces are at play big man but I just came around in your sleigh and it looks like today isn't my day to go'.

Paul then simply smiled at Santa but he had a defiant look in his eyes.

'Let's finish this' he declared.

And with that he joined in playing the most important rift in the world, as Mrs Clause's light grew stronger and stronger, until eventually Crnobog could not fight any longer and the light struck him, engulfing him completely until he fell to the floor.

Harry and Jess looked at each other and embraced. Tracey and Darren shared a kiss, as did all the elves who had just been reunited with their soulmates but Paul and Mr's Clause just stood still, as they watched on as Santa ran up to the crumpled Crnobog. He kneeled down by his side and looked in to his eyes as they began to fade out.

Santa spoke softly 'Stay with me'.

Crnobog looked up at him but now without any hate 'Brother. I will always lo....' But before he could finish his sentence he was gone.

Santa continued to kneel there for several moments before Mrs Clause and Paul walked up to him and both put their hands on his shoulders.

'We will find a him a place to rest' Mrs Clause assured him.

Santa said nothing he knew he didn't need to. As he pulled himself up, he looked out to all the cheering and turned to Mrs Clause.

'It is going to be quite the job to get this lot home'.

Epilogue

365 Days Later

'If you two do not get your backsides down these stairs in five seconds I will personally come up there and smack them both!'

'I think we better go down' Jess advised Harry as they sat on his bed.

'Yeah I don't really want my mum to beat me in front of you'.

Jess got up and turned towards Harry.

'Well that would be two of the women in your life that could kick your butt then'.

She laughed and quickly left the room followed by Harry. They both went down the stairs and in to his living room which was full of life. All of both of their families were there, Harry's mum and dad, Jess's mum and dad, who were now back together and even Harry's brother and sister had returned home for Christmas with their partners. They all cheered as the pair of them entered the room which was filled top to toe with Christmas decorations covering every last inch.

'Well nice for you two to make an appearance' Harry's mother quipped, walking up to them.

Harry's brother tried to defend them 'Hey give them a break mum their young and in love'.

'Not on Christmas eve they're not' She retorted.

She kissed both Harry and Jess on their cheeks.

'Now do the pair of you want snowballs?'

'Yes' They both replied simultaneously.

Harry's mum went off to make the pair of them drinks. Just as she left, Harry's three-year-old niece came running up to him, calling out his name, so he scooped her up.

'Uncle Harry it's Christmas eve'.

'Oh, I know isn't it great. Now have you been a good girl for Santa?'

She nodded vigorously 'Yeah I promise'.

'Well that's good. That means you should get all the presents you asked for then'.

Her face lit up and her big blue eyes widened just imaging all the presents she was about to get.

'Yes, and now daddy needs to put you to bed, doesn't he? Because the sooner you go sleep, the sooner Santa will come'

Harry passed his niece back to his brother. He opened the door but before he left, he leaned in to the pair of them and whispered.

'Don't you just love it when they're at this age and still believe in Santa. Sometimes I wish I still did'. He chuckled and walked out the door.

Jess and Harry looked at each other and smiled, they were lucky, they would never forget and on this Christmas eve and all those to come they would know it was extra special and they would love it just as much as Harry's niece did. As they knew, Christmas really was the most wonderful time of the year.

Over at the north pole Santa stood at the open barn doors looking out across the snowy landscape. He took a moment to think about his brother. Knowing he was truly gone forever he missed him, they had brought him back here to bury at the north pole and all Santa could do was hope that now his brother could find peace.

The barn doors to the side swung open, unapologetically interrupting Santa's moment of reflection, and their stood Mrs Clause.

'You ready to rock?' She asked emphatically.

'Well we must keep to schedule, can not be upsetting Paul now can we' Santa sarcastically replied as he waked towards the sleigh.

'He lives for you to stress him out, he is in the control centre now with Tracey and Darren going through the time schedule. Luckily I managed to escape by point sixty-three thank heavens.'

Santa laughed at the remark as he got in to the sleigh and Mrs Clause huddled in next to him.

'Are you sure you want to come along? It is a really long night ahead'.

'Do you really think I am going to let you do this one alone after everything. You know me better than that. Besides I did raise actual hell for you, I think that gives me at least one sleigh ride on Christmas eve'.

'I guess it does to be fair to you'.

Santa looked forward at all of the reindeer, who were now all perfect specimens again, well all except for John who was now looking on from his stable at them.

'On Rudolph, on Dasher, on Prancer, on Vixen, on Comet, on Cupid, on Dancer, on Donner, on Blitzen!'

Santa whipped the reigns, the sleigh and reindeers launched in to the night sky and out the north pole portal, off to deliver Christmas presents once more.

THE END

Printed in Great Britain
by Amazon